Sapphire Kill

J.J. Sweed

Dedicated to Jennifer and Curtis Sweed. Without you guys, this would have never come to be.

"I can see it right in front of me

But something is saying no.

Granted a lot has come to me

But sum' major ideas still trying make it go.

Fortune Force Field.

I can taste it but can't drink

I can make it when I think it

Can't mistake it, so distinctive

Man, I hate this, man I dreamed it, can't believe it

I gotta' let it go!

- Tech N9ne

"Maybe it erupted from an ocean trench, you know? Or a crevasse. Crevice. It's just a theory. I mean, for all we know, it's from another planet and it flew here."

- Cloverfield

"Then I stood on the sand of the sea. And I saw a beast rising up out of the sea, having seven heads and ten horns, and on his horns ten crowns, and on his heads a blasphemous name."

- Revelation 13:1

Part One: Life, Then Comes Death

My name is Michael Anthony Thompson, and I am writing to tell what happened on New Year's Eve night, 2013. My friends and I have been moving from one area to another almost every month. A man, who is no longer with us, said I should tell my story to help release stress and anxiety. Perhaps it might keep me sane while these things are still here and happening. My friends are still keeping their heads together by joking and telling stories which has also helped. They kept saying it was dead, but were always wrong. I guess it would help if I started from the beginning.

I was born a healthy infant on January 13th, 1995. My mother, Janice Tiffany Lark Thompson, said that I was her only one she planned on having. She didn't want to go through the hell of child birth again, but felt blessed when she had me all the same. My father, Lucas James Thompson, wanted another, but my mother put a stop to those thoughts before he really even had them. My parents met in college through a roommate. My father was studying Business a year above my mother who was studying agriculture at Texas A&M. There was a party and Anthony Perks introduced my dad to my mom, and they said there was a spark that went off in their brains that said he/she was the one. They dated until both had graduated, then my dad finally popped the question to my mom. Then, a short five months after being married my mom got pregnant. She was offered a C-section, but turned down the offer. "Worst mistake," she said. My parents decided to name me after my grandfather, Michael Lark and after Anthony Perks for making this all come true.

My dad and mom decided to move to Houston when I was two, after my dad had saved enough money to live in a good neighborhood. He was also promised a job transfer for an oil company as one of the managers. Better pay, better hours. After a week of living in a new home, a family down the street came over to say hello. It was two black ladies one looking older than the other and a little boy already walking. "Hi, I'm Janet Jones and this is my sister, Rose. The little one is my son, Matthew." My mother, smiling, shook everyone's hand, not worrying about being sweaty from doing a little work around the house.

"We saw your little boy and were wondering if he would like someone to play with? All Matthew does at home is eat, sleep, and watch television."

"Of course!" replied my mom.

From then on, Matt and I were basically like brothers, always arguing which one would be the adopted one. Even at school, we couldn't be separated. We picked each other for projects, teammates for gym, and sat at lunch together. By the time middle school came around, Matt was starting to become friends with just about everybody. He still made tons of time for me of course, but I wasn't like him. I was that shy kid that liked to write poems in the back corner of class. One day, in my math class, the teacher wanted us to partner up to do fractions or something like that. Matt had a different math class than I did, so it made things ten times more awkward. Everyone was paired up except me and the new girl that moved from Mississippi. I asked if I could work alone, as did the new girl. The teacher said everyone must be paired up to make the fraction problem work out right and told me to move my desk next to hers. She looked nervous, so I held out my hand first to shake. She smiled and I thought she was going to laugh at me, but instead she shook it and said her name was Rachel Marie. She was absolutely beautiful, but I knew it would make things weird if I told her that right away. After that day, Rachel and I have been partners for all the math projects.

Soon enough, Rachel started to hang out with Matt and me. She told us that her parents were killed in a car accident when she was three and she ended living with her grandparents. When her grandfather died when she was about 11 or so, her grandmother thought it would be best for her to live with a relative that wasn't as old; which is how she came to live with her uncle in Houston. He's a lieutenant in the Marines newly stationed in the Houston area. She's lived with him for six years now.

Throughout middle school, Rachel slowly came out from under her shell and socialized more with others. Especially with Brock Baxton. Rachel ended up dating Brock our freshman year of high school. I was fine with it. Wouldn't necessarily say I was happy about it, but he seemed to make her happy so whatever. That is until I saw bruises on her face and arms and instantly knew the one hundred forty-five pound quarterback had something to do with them. She pleaded with me to not do anything stupid, but I did. How could I not? I went up to Brock and socked him square in the jaw. It was the only punch I was able to get in before his buddies jumped in. I was suspended for four days; it was the best thing the principal could think of knowing I'm an all A-student. My mom was furious with me, but my dad understood my explanation and just told me to not try to take care of it by myself next time. He would later teach me how to fight. Rachel broke up with Brock after that incident and came after school those four days to check up on me. Matt asked why I didn't want his help, but all I could tell him was that it just wasn't his fight.

From then on, Rachel, Matt, and I were great friends regardless of other people in our lives. That pretty much sums up what was going on in my life until the day before New Year's Eve of 2013. Nothing too special about my life, but it was working for me and I was happy overall.

Matt and I were playing a basketball game on my Xbox while blasting Journey's "Who's Crying Now" on my stereo. My mom yelled and told me to turn it down, so I got up to shut my door and realized that I forgot to pause the game and saw Matt got three points. He looked at me with a devilish smile and I just shook my head. I went to sit down and Matt looked around me and nodded his head. I turned around to see what he had indicated to find Rachel standing in my doorway.

"Don't know how to knock?" I asked.

"Didn't hear me come up the stairs?"

"If I did I wouldn't have shut the door."

She looked at me wanting to laugh but instead said, "Journey, classic." She grabbed a magazine and sat on my bed.

As she flipped through the pages she asked me, "Who is this band?"

I looked at the magazine. "Daft Punk. They're like a techno group." She made a sound meaning that she understood. I paused the game and went to my CD collection and pulled out *Discovery* by Daft Punk.

"Wanna listen?" She nodded, then I looked at Matt.

"It's your house." he said. I opened the stereo to put the CD in. Matt and I continued playing our game and I looked back to see Rachel smiling and bobbing her head in enjoyment.

"'One More Time' is the name of the song."

"I like it. You guys want to go to the roof?" Right before she said that, Matt had beaten me in our game.

"What was that? I couldn't hear you over the crowd yelling my name," Matt said. She pointed up and we knew what she meant.

The roof of my house was made as if someone intended to watch the sunsets from it. Which, Rachel and I did many times, just us, talking until we were blue in the face. Matt and I had our fair share of talks on the roof, too. It was like an open sanctuary. When my dad found out that I went up there, he decided to build a ladder that connected my window to the roof so it would be easier to climb up there. He didn't even give me a safety talk, just said to use it wisely, he was good like that.

It was only about four thirty and the sun wouldn't be going down for another three hours or so. We talked about the party that my parents were going to have for New Year's. They said it was going to be a lot of family and friends (of my parents that is), but they said I could have a few friends of my own. Mainly so I wouldn't be alone with my older cousins who might be drinking. After the incident with Brock, the only friends I'd cared to be around were the ones I was sitting on the roof with.

"Don't be so dramatic, Mike. What about those guys in your chemistry class," said Matt.

"Who, the teacher and student teacher?" I said wanting to laugh.

"Oh, right, well shit, looks like you're stuck with me and the one with the pair of boobs that isn't your mom."

"Gee, thanks for that," Rachel said.

"You're welcome," Matt said. We all laughed, but then I started thinking about if all this would last, and I guess Rachel saw that I looked disgruntled.

"You alright, Mike?" I didn't look at her, but I heard what she said.

I finally asked them, "Do you think we will stay friends for a long time?" I looked up and saw Matt and Rachel look at each other then they busted out laughing.

"Where did that come from? I think you answered your own question," Matt said putting his arm around me. "I believe so, not sure about the chick next to me though," he got closer to me and whispered, "She always seemed sketchy to me. It's a girl's mind power that could get you killed."

"I heard that fucker. Mike, I'll be your friend 'til I'm dead. No doubt." That made me feel better. A lot better to be honest. "Now

Matt on the other hand, if he keeps acting like an asshole then I might have to kill him and then he wouldn't be here to be your friend anymore."

"See, prime example. Women will kill somebody just to prove they are right." We both started laughing, and Matt nodded his head and finally laughed at himself.

"What made you think that?" Rachel asked.

"I don't know. I guess I've just had a lot on my mind."

"Uh oh, is it time for a Dr. Marie session? Spill out all your secrets."

I laughed then took a deep breath and straightened up, "When I became friends with Matt I was too young to remember it, and now he's a familiar face that I've gotten used to having around all the time. I remember becoming friends with you three years ago, but even then we were pushed together by a teacher. My point is, I don't know what I'm going to do when high school is over. You two are the only ones I talk to."

Rachel had this look on her face like she was thinking very hard about what I had just said. She got up then gave me a hug, "We'll always be in touch somehow, whether by phone or some stupid social media site that's relevant when we're out of high school. But even then, you will still have to push yourself to meet new people and make new friends. Now if you did something about your long, nappy hair, then you would get some more attention."

"Not going to happen."

"Okay, but don't say I didn't warn you," she said with a smirk.

There was a honk down below us and it was Rachel's uncle. She gave him a wave, "Alright guys I'll see y'all later." And, after a couple of quick hugs, she climbed down the ladder.

Then, I thought of something and went after her, "Wait up." I met her inside. I went to my stereo and got out the Daft Punk CD then put it in the case and said, "I'll let you borrow it."

She looked at it waiting for me to say psych or just joking then she took it, "Thanks, Mike." I heard her say goodbye to my mom, and my mom responding by making sure she was coming to the party and inviting her uncle as well.

"I'm sure he would love to come, and I will definitely be here tomorrow. Bye."

"Buh bye, sweetie." I heard the door close.

"Why doesn't your mom call me *sweetie*?" Matt asked coming through the window.

"Do I really need to answer that? Come here, I need to show you something." I went to my drawer and dug under my boxers and pulled out a small box. I handed it to Matt who looked surprised when he opened it.

"You plan on marrying someone or something? Legally speaking, you're about a year too young for that."

"No, I plan on giving Rachel this tomorrow night. But look more closely." He got up closer.

"Is that a blue rock in the ring?"

"Sapphire, it's her birthstone." He made a sound that let me know he understood.

"How much this thing cost? An arm? Possibly a leg?"

"Close, it was around nine hundred or so."

"What the hell are you doing spending that much on a female? Wait… You asked those questions for a reason didn't you? To see if it was worth giving it to her?"

I applauded him, "Nicely done, Matthew."

"I know, I even surprise myself sometimes."

I felt my phone vibrate in my pocket. It was a text from my dad and if I remember correctly it said, "On my way from work. Thinking about ordering Pizza Hut. I'm assuming Matt is there so I would need to double my order."

"Oh yes sir you do." Matt said looking over my shoulder.

"Bro, you're in my bubble." He stepped back some and I responded to my dad saying Matt was here and go ahead with the double.

I got a reply saying, "Alrighty, I'll see you as soon as this traffic clears up."

It's almost 2014 and we still can't figure out a way to fix the traffic jams at rush hour, was the thought that ran through my head while I waited for the pizza to arrive. Matt fell on my bed holding a *Rolling Stone* magazine that he flipped through for a second before he asked, "Is the food here yet?"

Almost an hour passed before my dad arrived with the pizza. Matt always seemed to be hungry yet still managed to rock a six pack. This concerned my mom and she would ask me from time-to-time if he had been around a certain plant. I always just told her that if he was she would be asking the same about me since we were together so much. I would get that look from her that said *you better be joking* and then I would kiss her on the cheek and tell her not to worry. Mom handed out paper plates to everyone, while Matt handed out paper towels, and my dad opened the boxes of pizza. It was still warm.

To think about it now, I would actually kill for some pizza. All I've had for the past few days is canned beans and canned pork chops. I never even knew that there was pork chops in a can. Sometimes, I wonder if there is still a grocery store that still has fresh food, but I know most of it has been shipped out by the military.

Matt and I ate the pizzas like there was no tomorrow, so dad used it the perfect to ask Matt some questions. "So are you coming to help get the house ready for the party tomorrow?" My parents were planning to decorate the house with balloons and streamers and other shit that would be super tacky.

"Uh, yea-" Matt caught himself through a bite of pizza, "Yes, sir, what time should I be over?"

"Around noon would be nice."

"Noon, got it."

I leaned over to Matt and whispered, "Kill me now." He handed me another slice of pizza and I gladly took it.

When we were done and disposed the garbage, I told my parents that I was going to walk Matt home. We walked out and the temperature was still around the mid-seventies, that's Texas for you. I rolled up my sleeves and felt an instant relief.

"Dude, I feel like I'm carrying a baby," Matt said holding his bloated stomach.

"Is it kicking?" he laughed a sarcastic laugh.

"Once I get home I am crapping this baby right out."

I heard something that sounded like thunder and looked up, but there wasn't a cloud in the sky. I assumed it was a big truck passing a couple blocks away. We reached Matt's house and I could hear Family Feud on the television, the one with Steve Harvey as the game host. Matt's mom was yelling out, "Prostitute! Prostitute!" followed by a roar of laughter.

"Well, that show should keep them occupied for at least another two hours. Enough time for me to use the phone to get my mack on."

"You still don't have a cell phone that works?"

"Nah, my auntie keeps the phone bill up with her lover from Paris or some shit."

"Well, call me around ten so I can be sure you didn't bail on coming at noon."

"Couldn't if I tried, Mom and auntie going to Conroe to see my family for New Years. I told them that you were throwing a party and said I could go, but would have to see if I could stay the night at your place. My mom might lend me her cell phone tomorrow, maybe."

"I'm sure you can stay the night. Especially, if you come and help out tomorrow." I felt my phone vibrate again but ignored it.

"I will, I will. Later man."

"See ya," I said as he walked in the house. I heard that sound of a big truck passing again, but this time it sounded a lot closer. As I was walking back, I checked my phone and stopped to see it was Rachel who had texted and it read, "My uncle already knew about your little shindig your parents are having... Wonder who could have told him?" She added a smiley face at the end, but I was positive that I didn't tell her uncle about the party.

I heard little bells clanging and saw it was the Stoopings from a couple houses down and there little Yorkie, Shelia. Both were former doctors. They've helped my family whenever we had some sort of flu or virus ever since we moved in the neighborhood. Mr. Stooping is also a really great singer; he would go to my birthday parties and sing old jazz songs. Every time I remember those songs now, it gives me chills.

I continued reading the text, "Anyways my uncle took me shopping and he found me a pretty little dress. So, I guess I'm getting all dressed up for a change." This made me laugh, because I wasn't used to seeing Rachel in a dress at all. She considered herself a Tomboy and the only time she dressed up was at our ninth grade homecoming when she went with Brock.

There was another thunderous boom and this time it sounded like it was right behind me. I heard Mr. Stooping ask his wife, "Did you hear that?" When I walked across the street there was a flash of light and my hearing was instantly lost along with my vision. I was lying on the ground holding my ears as the ringing sound continued to get louder. I kept blinking uncontrollably to get the black spots our of my view, and that's when I started to panic. I figured I stepped on a bomb or something, so I felt my body all over to make sure everything was still intact. When my vision was coming to, I saw a little furry creature running towards me. I could hear it yapping but the sound was still muffled. When things started to clear, I saw an old man standing in front of me.

"Are you fall-right?" is what I heard.

"Huh?"

"Are you alright?"

"Yeah, I'm fine I-I don't know what happened. Did I step on a land mine or something?" The old man, which turned out to be Mr. Stooping, let out a little chuckle, "No, son, you were almost struck-"

"Jesus H. Christ!" That I heard, and knew instantly it was my dad. "Michael, son, are you hurt?"

"No, Dad," I let out a reassuring chuckle, "I think I'm fine."

"Mark, did you see what happened?" my dad asked.

"Saw the whole thing…your son was almost struck by what appeared to be lightning."

"What, but there isn't a cloud," he said, as he looked up and paused to stare at one dark purple cloud hovering right over us. I remember looking at it, wondering how one cloud could cause so much damage and confusion. The air was still in a way that would make you feel like you should stop breathing.

"Holy crap, Mike," Matt said coming out of his house wearing an under shirt and sweat pants, "I was using the bathroom when I heard a boom, that I though came from me!" This made me laugh harder than I expected and helped to calm me down. He bent over to help me up as my dad did the same for Mr. Stooping, who was a little shorter than my dad mainly from hunching over all the time.

"Will he be alright?" my dad asked Mr. Stooping.

"I expect he'll be fine, a little shook up is all. Just watch his breathing, and, son, if you start to feel your heart race or the ringing in your ears doesn't let up tell someone ok? Can you make it home alright?"

"Yes, sir, I can make it."

I told Matt I would see him tomorrow and walked back to my house with my dad holding my elbow just in case. My mom was standing in the doorway wringing her hands and biting her lip. When I reached the yard, she ran out and hugged me. Before she could ask, I told her I was fine, "Just my head hurts is all." She walked me back inside and gave me some aspirin.

That night, I woke up sweating, gasping for air. I brushed the hair out of my face and looked at the clock which read 4:36 AM. I laid my head back down and started feeling cold. I opened my eyes again due to the streetlight outside that was annoying flickering on and off. This was starting to give me a headache, again. Even with my eyes shut I was aware of the light, struggling on its last bit of life. *On, Off, On, Off.....* It irritated me to the point where I had to get up to shut my blinds. Before I closed them, I looked at the spot where God had almost struck me down. I stared at the spot for a good two minutes examining the crack that started from the lightning initially hit and traveled along the road all the way to the beginnings of a yard. The light started flickering faster. Then, it finally blew out.

I laid back down, and tossed for a bit before I fell asleep again. I woke up and the sun was out and the smell of bacon was in the air. The clock read 8:16 AM. I got up, stretched and proceeded downstairs. My dad was reading the newspaper and put it down when I came into the room. "Hey sparky," he said.

"Hun, don't say that. How do you feel sweetheart?"

"I'll feel better after some bacon," I said.

"And eggs and sausage," my dad added.

I really need to stop remembering the food I ate then, it just upsets me.

Finished eating, I headed to the restroom to pee when my phone went off. Matt had sent me a text to a link from the channel three news website that indicted there had been weird cloud formations around different parts of Texas and other parts of the country that were causing random bursts of lightning. He sent me a follow up text saying, "Crazy shit right?"

My bladder was telling me I had a few seconds before I would explode, so I made it to the bathroom and felt a great rush of fluid exit my body. When I washed my hands something dawned on me. I dried my hands quickly and went to text Matt to see if he told Rachel about what happened last night and he said he was just about to. I texted, "It might be best if I told her later."

"How late is later?"

"Soon," I thought about it then typed, "after the party."

I set my phone down and put some work clothes on. When Matt showed up he was wearing a shirt that was kind of big on him with a fading picture of Obama and Martin Luther King and what was meant to say *Fulfilling the Dream* but was missing a few letters My dad came up behind me and checked his watch, "11:58 AM. Not bad. You guys ready?"

"Let's do this!" Matt said, but came out *Let'z do thees.*

It was four o'clock in the afternoon by the time we finished, and I was wiped out. Matt went back to his house to shower and get ready, and I went upstairs to do the same thing. There's a radio that hung by the door in the bathroom that I switched on to listen to the talk shows. I liked listening to the political debates and the religious freaks. I am Catholic, but it was always entertaining how some Jesus fanatics freak out over the little things. But the show that was on that day was the most frightening I'd ever listened to. I had caught the guy in the middle of his rant, but what I heard I can still remember…

"…heed the Word. The Word cries of a beast from the seas. It will devour your souls and leave you in unbearable pain, the worst you will ever experience. Repent now in the name of the Father, Son, and Holy Spirit. This will be the end of my service for the Savior is on his way. God Bless you all, and may He have mercy on your soul!"

Then, it cut off to a weather warning signal. There was a thunderstorm on its way to the area. I ignored the weather warning and was reflecting on what the religious guru had just said. I kept thinking that they must have fired him or something to make him say something like that. At that moment, because I wasn't focusing on actually taking a shower, I got soap in my eye. Irritated, I rinsed off and got out.

May He have mercy on your soul.

My parents had said this party was going to be a formal occasion and when I asked how formal my mom went to my closet and pulled out my suit and told me to figure out the rest. I ironed my shirt and pants and felt the heat still clinging to them when I put them on. Relaxing into the clean, warmth I was comforted a bit, but it wasn't enough to make me forget the cold words from the radio DJ I had heard earlier.

…mercy on your soul.

I took a glance in the mirror, and was surprised to notice that I looked pretty good. I went to my drawer and pulled out the box that contained the sapphire ring. I slipped it into my suit pocket right as someone was knocking on my bedroom door. Before I could answer it, Matt, in a tan suit with a black button up shirt and jeans, walked in. He was holding a bow tie and asked, "Should I wear this?"

"With that outfit? No."

"Thanks, I fucking hate getting dressed up for parties."

"Tell me about it, I have to wear this freaking suit and can't figure out which tie to pair with it."

He looked over my shoulder, "What about that one?"

I looked over and saw he was talking about my grandfather's tie I received last Christmas as a twisted reminder that he was being buried six feet under in a different state at the same time. I thought about it and went to pick it up. I never wore it, but I remember my grandpa being a sharp dresser and him telling me how he wore this tie – or something similar – when he met my grandmother. And, if I was planning to give Rachel a gift that might mean something for us in the future...*Why not?* I thought. I turned to Matt to get his opinion and he gave me a thumbs up. "Anyone else here?" I asked

"A few people. Six or seven at the most. How many people are your parents expecting?"

"Dunno, Mom said her side of the family and friends. Same for my dad."

"And how can you forget me?" Rachel said walking into my bedroom.

I had never seen Rachel the way she looked before that night. Maybe at that one homecoming years ago, but I think I've already mentioned that. She was like a beautiful princess without the tiara. Her dress was a mix of black and purple, she had curled the tips of her hair, and even had make up on. Make up! She was always going on about being all natural and normally I agreed and thought she was pretty with or without all the glam, but now… I was speechless. Thank God Matt finally said something, "Don't lose your glass slipper, Cinderella. You might get your evil, step sister's blood in it."

"Thanks, you look nice too, Matt, and all your Grimm story references."

"You look amazing," damn it, I hoped that didn't shoot me up the creepy scale.

She responded with, "Aww, thank you Mike. You're looking snazzy yourself, especially your tie. Is it vintage?"

"It was grandfather's, so yeah."

"And another ten points to me for being right," she said, as she made a tally in the air. Rachel said that my mom was expecting us downstairs soon. As much as I didn't want to mingle with my parent's friends, I figured it would make things less awkward with Rachel and me.

Downstairs, Rachel's uncle had some interesting stories about when he was in training for the Marines. He said that it wasn't like what you see in the movies at all. "The pain is actually experiencing it while not knowing if it's even possible for you to make it through, but it's all worth it in the end." Then, his phone started to ring and he excused himself. Rachel continued his story and explained how he was stationed in Iraq where it was so hot that your boots would melt to the ground if you stayed in one place for too long. "This was when I was with my Mimi. She would always worry about him. Saying little prayers and all that jazz." Rachel's uncle had come back in the room almost speed walking and had a little terror in his eyes.

"Sweetie, I have to go, something urgent has come up. If I'm not back ask one of the Thompsons to give you a ride home."

"Is everything alright?"

He kissed her on top of the head, "Don't worry, kiddo." He walked over to my Dad, shook his hand, told him thanks for inviting him, and said he had an urgent call and hoped to make it back in time for the countdown. Rachel watched her uncle walk out the door, then looked at the floor.

"You alright?" I asked her.

She brought up her head lighting fast, "Huh, oh yeah, I'm fine. Couldn't wait to get away from him," she said with a sarcastic smile.

The night went on and we kept talking and listening to music from my parents' teenage years. Stevie Nicks' "Edge of Seventeen," Prince's "1999," Journey's "Don't Stop Believing," Mötley Crüe's "Kickstart My Heart," Poison's "Talk Dirty To Me," and the list goes on from there. It was 11:35 PM and I saw that Rachel was getting a little worried. I patted her on the shoulder and told her to come to my room, "There's something I want to give you." She smiled and got to her feet and followed me.

This is it. This will finally show my feelings for her, I thought. I was starting to sweat and get fidgety with my emotions at an all-time high. I had never felt the way I did that night. I wish it could have gone better.

We reached my room and I when Rachel turned to face me I took her hands. "I hope this doesn't make things weird between us, but when we got paired up that one day in math something in my brain turned on. To be honest I was a little skeptical at first, but the more we talked… I never thought I would become such great friends with someone as amazing as you." She was starting to blush and looked away, but when our eyes connected again I said, "I want to give you something…"

She looked past me to the window and her face went slack. She dropped my hands and went towards the window, "What is that? What the hell is that?" I looked out the window, but I didn't see anything. "No, I know I saw something," she said, as she started climbing the ladder. When I reached her on the roof, there was fear in her eyes. I saw what she pointed at. It was a plane caught on fire and falling from the sky nose first. There was an earthquake, or at least what felt like one, that almost shook us off the roof. We grabbed for each to steady ourselves and I said that we had to climb back down.

"What the fuck is that?" she screamed out with such terror that I was almost afraid to look myself. It was walking on four legs and it let out a screeching yell. It was as big as a skyscraper and there were horns sticking out from the top of its head and bottom of its jaw. The creature had a shiny skin or scales, I wasn't really sure which, and it looked as if it had just come out of the water, There were helicopters circling the thing, shining its lights on it trying to shoot it down.

From where I was standing, I could see that many people were shocked frozen by the beast standing on roofs and hoods of cars. I tugged on Rachel's hand more firmly and we finally went back inside.

We ran back downstairs and I went to my dad trying to tell him what we saw, but he hushed me and turned up the television. The news anchor was more frightened than we were. She kept fading in and out, but I understood most of what she said, "I am just getting informed that we need everyone to evacuate the city and head north to the nearest area with military force. From there the military-" She was caught off from the power outage and the ground was trembling again.

My dad yelled out, "Ok people you heard her, we need everyone to get to their cars and drive north from here."

"Where further north are these military forces?" someone shouted.

"I know exactly where the place they're wanting us to go, I just need everyone to get in their cars and just follow me," my dad said.

I looked over and saw my mom putting stuff into a trash bag. Everyone else was heading outside, but I went over to my mom and told her that we had to go. "I'm coming, you get Matthew and Rachel in the car with your father."

"But what about yo-"

"DO IT!" she said with fear in her voice.

So, I grabbed Rachel's hand and pushed Matt out the door with us following behind. Outside, there was a burning smell in the air. We piled in the car and we saw my mom run out with a sack that looked like what Santa Clause would carry around. She popped the trunk to the car and threw the stuff in then ran around to the front to get in. We backed up into the street where there were cars lined up waiting anxiously. We were scared, but we didn't exactly know what to be scared of. I mean what was that thing and where did it come from?

We drove quickly, when we could, and we passed by houses were people were panicking and putting stuff into their vehicles. There was a mother holding her child on the side of the road waving her arms around trying to catch a ride. We drove by her and I wish I hadn't of looked back at her, because we saw her unexpectedly run down by a car that didn't stop until it crashed into the house behind her. I was breathing heavily and my dad yelled at me to turn around and put my seat belt on, but I just couldn't move. Rachel shook my shoulder and I snapped out of it and turned around. There were houses and lawns on fire with no one tending to them. People yelling things like *We're dead!* and *Hurry the fuck up!* I remember hearing, "Where's little Derrick? WHERE IS MY BABY?" screamed over and over again. There were people on their knees with their heads bowed and praying then and others that were going into shock and breaking out into seizures. Once we reached the highway the chaos only got worse. People who weren't in cars were running alongside them or banging on windows trying to gain access inside. One woman tripped and nobody stopped for her they just trampled over her.

"What's going on? Lucas? Terrorists?" my mom asked in a shaky voice. My dad just kept driving, rubbing his forehead the only indication that he heard her speak. I looked at Rachel and she nodded at me to say something.

I started, "Mom, Rachel and I saw some-"

"Shhh…" Dad said, as he turned up the radio.

"The National Guard has advised all citizens to head toward north and to stay away from Downtown. There is a...a…something attacking us. Uh, I don't really know what, but I have to get out of here. We all have to get out of here and-" It cut off to another emergency broadcast announcing more earthquake-like tremors, which we were already feeling. The jolts made my dad swerve a little, but he soon got the car under control and sped up when he could. Behind us, others were not as fortunate as we heard tires screeching and collisions in progress.

Matt's phone rang and he looked surprised. He answered, "Hello mom," he listened and his face looked like he had been punched in the stomach. He ended the call and I whispered over to him, "Is everything all right?"

He kept looking down, "That was my uncle." He took a deep breath and continued, "My mom, the roof collapsed and she was crushed under it. She's…dead." A single tear ran down his cheek. That was the first time I saw Matt cry and I wasn't sure how to handle it, but Rachel already had her arm around him.

There were more tremors, this time bigger than the others. It made my dad swerve again. Rachel, Matt, and I held on to each other. I didn't open my eyes, not even a little just kept them squeezed shut. There was a sound of glass shattering and my dad yelled, "Holy shit, Oh my god!"

Then we hit something and there was more breaking glass. The car came to a sudden halt. After mentally checking to see if I was alright, I slowly, slowly opened my eyes. I wish I hadn't. There was a sign pole going through the windshield and…my mom. I couldn't even think about what I was seeing. She was slumped over the pole, blood oozing out from the edges of the fatal wound.

I knew she was dead, her eyes told me so. Tears flooded my eyes. I looked to Rachel and Matt and their faces registered the same shock that must have been on mine, but then Mike pointed to the driver's seat. Directly in front of me was a gaping hole in the windshield. He was lying on the ground twenty feet in front of the car and not moving.

"Dad! Daaad!" I hollered as I struggled to get out of the stupid seatbelt. I ran him. Shook him, but he never answered me. His head was crushed on one side where he hit the pavement. In one moment, my parents had been taken from me. I sobbed into my father's shoulder as I pulled him close. How could I move on from this?

"Mike?" Rachel said, but it was all muffled, like when I almost got struck by lightning. She continued on, "I'm really, really sorry Mike, but we can't stay here. We have to go. Mike?" My eyes were filled with tears and she gave me a quick hug. Then Matt opened the door and got out. Rachel pulled on my hand, but I couldn't move. My body was numb. The ground started to shake again, enough to loosen my hold on Dad's lifeless body. I let Matt and Rachel peel my arms free from him. We grasped each other until the earthquake subsided, then we started moving.

I wiped the tears and put the images out of my mind that would haunt me the rest of my life. There was a crowd running past us and we joined it not knowing what else to do. A tank went by on the other side of the road, pushing cars and bodies out of its way, in the direction of the beast, and I could only pray for its death.

After a bit of running, I just couldn't take it anymore I had to stop for a break. My breath was coming in great heaves and I dropped to my knees to try and slow it. As I did, I felt the small box on the inside of my chest pocket. I took it out and moved it to my pants pocket, thinking the person who bought that ring was someone who used to have parents. The images I had squashed for long enough to get us off the road, rose up unbidden and with them I vomited up the last of party food.

"Let's just wait right here for a second," I said, trying to control my sobs and my heaving breath. Matt nodded and so did Rachel. "What was that thing?"

"I think it was some kind of monster, but I have no idea," replied Rachel.

"Are you mental? What do you mean monster? I thought this was terrorists." Matt said trying to catch his breath.

"No, Rachel and I were standing on the roof when the...Thing was attacking the city."

"What? Seriously? Well, shit," he paused and then looked up and I knew he wanted to cry.

"Where do we go? We can't stay here," said Rachel. I thought for a second and looked around. I got up and walked back to the road. The nearest road sign said that Dallas was 102 miles away and Ft. Worth 96 miles. I scratched my head and remembered what that guy on the radio said about going towards the north.

"We head north. That way. That's where my...my...dad was going, so we keep that direction," I pointed and they looked. "I think if we keep going north we will find more people and safety, if not armed forces."

They looked at each other and Rachel said, "Okay, I trust you to lead the way." And she put her hand on my shoulder.

We looked at Matt, but when he opened to say something there was an explosion. We all jumped. "Shit I'm down, let's get the hell out of here," and with that he started running north.

That night we ran for at least three miles in our dress outfits. Once we got outside the city chaos, we walked. That whole night we never saw a car with someone driving it. When came across a gas station, we went inside to look for food and a television or radio to see if there were any updates.

But when we opened the door the smell of blood and rotting flesh hit us and we could hear the buzzing of flies. We walked to the drink aisle and saw all the water was gone. All that was left was a few sodas and beers. I thought about taking the beer and forgot about it knowing it would only make my stomach more upset. At the end of the aisle, there was a body lying on the ground. There were bullet wounds on his back and his head. Not too far from the first body, was another one that sat in a chair with the head blown off and a shotgun sitting between his legs. Rachel looked away and vomited, but quickly recovered with a stony-face glance around the convenient store. She picked up a nearby backpack and started stuffing it with supplies.

I walked around trying to find some kind of shirt. There was a shirt rack but most of the shirts were splattered in blood. I searched for one that had less stains than the others and managed to find one that said *I'm From Texas!* It was a large, a perfect size for me. I grabbed what I thought were the right sizes for Matt and Rachel, and then continued my search around the store.

There was a sound coming from the back. It was Matt who shouted, "I found some water back here." Rachel took him the back pack to load up with water.

"Hey look for a radio. We need to figure out what's happening," I told them.

"Got it," Rachel said.

I walked to the back office and heard a sound like a giant bee buzzing around. I knew it was the static of a radio, so I fully opened the door. Draped across the desk was another body, this one decapitated. My heart was beating faster, and it didn't matter how much I blinked I couldn't stop staring. *Who or what could have done that?* Matt came up behind me and prodded me to walk into the office. He saw the body and the look on my face and walked straight to the desk and grabbed the radio.

Back in the main room of the store, we tuned the radio to any frequency it would pick up. Finally, through the static we heard,

"I have just received word that Air Force One has crashed with the President, Vice President, and first Family in it. May god have mercy on-" It cut off and the emergency broadcast came back on. My body shook from what I just heard. *What would this country do without a leader? What other countries had lost leaders?* So many questions were filling my head and it felt like I was going to pass out.

"We need to keep moving," I said. Matt turned off the radio right as Rachel screamed. I turned around, almost giving myself a whiplash, to see a scorpion-like creature with a curved beak the size of an F-150 truck and wings on its back. The noise it made was similar to what I had heard in the back of the store. The thing aimed its tail and charged towards us. We dived and rolled out of the way and all managed to get out of its way, but the creature was coming back towards us.

I looked around and saw a hatchet hanging on the wall next to the fire extinguisher. The plan was to kill the creature, but instead we all ran out the doors and the hatchet was used to lock the door handles in place. The creature ran full force against the doors, almost breaking them but not quite. It backed up to run at the door again and this time it did break the doors, but its head and neck were almost completely severed by the broken glass. Already panting, we took off down the road.

We stopped to take a breather and I took off the backpack. I could feel my back full of sweat. I thought of that *I'm from Texas!* T-shirt and pulled it out to change. I went to take off my suit, but I was so sweaty I couldn't get my arms out of the sleeves. I slammed my arms down to get loose of the jacket and then threw the jacket on the ground, kicking it as it fell. I fell on my knees and just cried uncontrollably. Matt came by my side and put his hand on my shoulder and I could hear him starting to cry himself.

"It's okay, bro."

"No it's not, we're dead."

"You can't think like that. Rachel and I, we-" he took a deep breath in, "we need you the most. Maybe Rachel more than me, because you know, women," he said, letting out a little chuckle. Despite my tears I smiled.

"He's right," Rachel came closer, "How do you expect me to keep going on with this dimwit all by myself?"

"Is that term still accepted in this day in age?" Matt asked.

"I think anything goes now," I said getting back up. "Whatever those things are, the military will kill them. I know they will."

Those words still haunt me today. But I think I gave my friends hope for few days.

We continued on for a few more hours until we all felt exhausted. We found it weird that we hadn't run into any people yet, other than the dead ones. There was a sign on the highway that said there would be a Wal-Mart at the next exit. We all agreed it would be a good place to stay for the night, and we decided to all sleep in the sports section.

We reached the parking lot of Wal-Mart which was filled with empty cars. Some of them were on fire. Some were wrecked into each other and the cart return spots. There was a dead dog that looked like its insides were torn out through the mouth. I had to hold my breath after I saw that, because the smell was so bad. Matt was opening car doors and looking under the seats, and before I could ask what he was looking for he brought his head out of a truck holding a pistol. He handed it to me and said, "Here, you know how to use it better than me." When I was younger my dad took me hunting and taught me the fundamentals of proper use for a gun. Matt was always afraid to shoot living things he thought would later become his dinner. I took it from him and checked to see that it was loaded and the safety was on and stuck it in my waistband.

We entered the Wal-Mart and looked around and listened. There was no buzzing sound like at the gas station. So far, so good. We went to the fruit section to see if there was anything to eat. Everything looked rotten and covered in blood. Even the bread looked old. I thought about how it hadn't been a full day of this thing attacking us and I didn't understand how all the food could be spoiled already. We made our way to the sport section, when I had the idea to get a watch. I told them I was going to check the watches and took off around the corner. There was one remaining winding watch that was still ticking. The date on it was 01/01/14, so it was still working properly so I took it off the shelf and strapped it to my wrist.

The sport section looked like a tornado had come through it. We looked all around for a sleeping bag and only found two, both of which had Hello Kitty plastered all over them. Matt and I had grabbed both of them and unfolded them.

"We'll take turns keeping watch; two hours each turn. I found a working watch so we can keep track. I'll go first, who wants second shift?" Rachel raised her hand and I nodded. I looked around for a chair and saw a Texas Longhorn folding chair and grabbed it, took it out of its wrapping, and unfolded it. The short time it took me to set up the chair, Rachel and Matt had already fallen asleep.

As I sat there in the flickering lights, I fiddled with the loaded pistol. There was a moment were I even held it against my head. Acting like I was going to pull the trigger. But I caught a glimpse of Matt and Rachel. My two closest friends. Matt's words kept on playing in my head, *We need you the most.* I could feel the box in my pocket. I thought, *Last night was supposed to be special. Maybe it was never supposed to happen? Then why do I still have the box?* There were so many questions that I let Rachel sleep for an extra hour. As I sat there in the silence, I kept feeling like we were the last three people on the planet. That thought made me shiver. I checked my watch and it said 8:00 AM.

"Hey?" Rachel said turning over, "Is it almost my turn?"

"Yeah, I gave y'all extra time to sleep."

"Why'd you do that?"

"Lost track of time."

"No, you're thinking about something. Tell me."

I put my hand on the box and said, "There's nothing wrong, just I'm tired is all."

She looked at me with bloodshot eyes and got up. She came over and gave me a quick kiss on the cheek, "When you're ready to talk, just let me know, okay?" I smiled and nodded my head. She shoved me off the chair and sat down.

"Do you know how to use a gun?" She shook her head. I handed her the gun and showed her where the safety was located and told her simply how to cock, aim, and fire.

"What if I miss?"

"You probably will, but the first shot will wake me and then I won't miss." She smiled and tussled my hair like I was a little boy. I went to lie down and before I knew it I was asleep.

I remember my dream. We were still in the car and we were the only ones on the road. Everything was quiet but I knew everyone was talking. Then everyone stopped what they were doing and sat up straight. My mom and dad looked at me, but they had no eyes and the blood was streaming down their faces. The car was still in drive and I was yelling at my dad to watch the road, but I couldn't even hear myself. When we crashed I heard the full effect, and in real life, whatever that was now, I was awoken by Matt telling me he heard something.

I got up slowly and for a moment I didn't see him holding the gun in my face. I took it and listened and I did hear something. It sounded like the wings we heard back at the gas station. I got up to my feet and noticed Rachel was still asleep. "Stay with her," I told Matt. He knelt down next to her and I took the gun off safety. The closer I walked forward the louder the sound grew. I looked around the corner and saw it was a large black bird with a broken wing. I listened for anything else but that was the only noise I could hear.

I put the gun back on safety and looked at the bird closely. I knew it was in serious pain and there was nothing I could do to help. Except put it out of its misery. I looked on the shelves and saw a can of soup. It was the only large item left on the shelves. I grabbed it and held it tightly. The bird stopped flapping as if it knew what I was about to do. The poor creature's eyes searched frantically and flapped some more. I got down on my knees and told it, "I'm so sorry, but this is what it comes to." I put the can over my head and slammed down on top of the bird's head and it was dead instantly.

I walked back to where Matt and Rachel were, sad from what I was just forced to do, but not wanting to concern them with it. "False alarm, just a bird." Matt chuckled and told me he almost pissed on his self. I chuckled myself.

I checked my watch, it was midnight. "Did you want to get some more rest?"

He thought about it and said, "No, But let's give her a few more minutes." I nodded and he sat next to the chair.

"I woke up before it was my turn. I heard her crying," he told me.

"Did you ask her what's wrong?" I asked.

"Yeah, she said that she was scared. Scared of everything that was around her."

"What did she mean 'everything around her?'"

"I asked that, too. She said she felt the walls talking to her. Telling her to just end it all."

"Like suicide?"

"Yeah, I'm worried, Mike. For all of us."

"I am too, but this event that's going on it will all be over soon. It has to be."

"And if it's not over soon, what then?"

I thought about it and he put his head on top of his knees. I finally said, "We have to stay strong, all of us. There will be no time for fear because if we let that take over, then we lose. Everything."

He looked at me and smiled, "Who said that?"

"I did." Matt smiled and put his head back on his knees.

We let Rachel sleep for another thirty minutes and we just listened to the silence. When we woke her up she woke with a jerk, like she was having a bad nightmare. I apologized and told her it was time to find some other people and find out what was going on in the rest of the world. She rubbed her eyes which were still bloodshot, probably from the crying.

"Why don't we just eat a little bit of what we have?" Matt asked. I thought about it and my stomach made my decision for me. I sat back down while Matt pulled out the candy we had. We tried to eat slowly, but even then we finished in five minutes. We packed up what was still left and added a few random things from the store to our pack. We even changed into new clothes.

Back on the road, we walked a good three hours. It wasn't too hot, probably because there were clouds covering most of the sun, but we were still sweating. I looked over to Matt and he was looking up at the sky. I asked him what he was looking at. He replied, "Do you ever look at the sun and ask yourself, *What the hell am I doing*?"

We all laughed and I said, "Are you being serious? Because the answer would be blinding yourself." Times like that were the only comforting moments we had.

We continued down the road keeping our eyes out for other people, but it had started to rain. It wasn't too much rain, but it was getting to the point where we needed to find some shelter. Up ahead, there was a house on the side of the road. Matt and I went up to a window and looked in. It seemed empty, so we decided to go in especially since the door was unlocked. "Hello?" There was no answer so we set our stuff on the floor and started looking around. I went to the restroom to look for some towels so we could dry off. Going through the hallway, I examined the photos on the walls. Most were pictures of a white couple with children that looked like they were adopted. It was a girl around the age of twelve and a little boy around the age of six or seven, both had noticeably darker skin than their parents.

I reached the bathroom, noticing that this part of the house was the most trashed. I luckily found some clean towels in the cabinet, and I took them back to the living room and handed them out.

"Look at what I found," said Rachel, holding some canned beans.

"What if they're expired?" Matt asked.

"Canned beans don't expire. They're in cans doofus."

"I was kidding, bubble butt." Matt and I both snickered at his comment while Rachel just stood there holding the beans.

"Well, I guess I can eat all three of these cans if I have such a round ass," she said now smiling while ours faded away. "Yeah, that's what I thought."

We ate the beans as slowly as we could all of us quiet for a time. Rachel especially looked like she was thinking about something.

"Something wrong, Rachel?"

"Why haven't we seen anyone yet? Like, are we the only people left on this Earth?"

I thought about this seriously, and I couldn't for the life of me come up with an answer. It scared me. What *if* we were the last people on Earth? I kept looking at my beans, and then it hit me, "I think what happened was, we were late to get the message. I mean look at what happened yesterday, when we were driving we never ran into traffic, people in that gas station were dead and decaying. That or that thing had been eating those people, but when we heard that something was attacking it must have been coming from where we're heading. Which might be good, or it might be really bad. But…" I looked at Rachel, "we have to keep our heads together no matter what." I saw her eyes water up a little bit, then she looked away and nodded her head.

We finished our beans and it was still raining pretty hard. Every time I heard the lightning, I would jump as if it was striking right next to me again. I looked out the window hoping to see headlights or someone walking down the road. There was another crack of thunder and it practically made me jump out of my skin.

Rachel sat down beside me looked at me with her head cocked, "Are you scared of the storm?"

"No, just the lighting," I told her.

"Why?"

"Well," I let out a sigh, "two nights ago when you guys came over, I walked Matt to his place and I could've sworn it sounded like a big truck or something, but I was almost struck by lightning."

I saw her expression and it looked like she thought I was joking, "Seriously?"

"Ask Matt, he knows." I looked back out the window as she got up. I watched her walk up to him while he was messing with an old radio. She asked him about the event and he glanced at me quickly before relating the story to her in full.

"There was a hole where it happened, in the road." She looked at him, then to me, finally to the floor. Her hands went behind her head as if she didn't know what to say.

"What if this was some kind of sign?" she asked.

"What do you mean?" I asked.

"Like, what if those things came from like space or something and it came down in the lightning, sort of like that War of the Worlds movie with Tom Cruise?"

I was trying to comprehend what she was trying to explain and when I went to look out the window I saw lights down the dark road. My eyes widened and I ran to the door. Outside the rain hit me with a force like I was running through a monsoon. I went out on the road and started waving my hands hoping the vehicle would see me. The car was coming really fast and didn't seem to be slowing down. I stood there like a deer caught in the headlights. It was close enough that I thought I could read the license plate. I held out my hands out praying it would stop, when Matt tackled me out of the way, and I heard the car speed past us.

"What the hell was that?" I asked.

"That was a car that didn't seem to care for pedestrians," he said. He helped me up and I thanked him for saving me. He nodded and we walked back to the house. Never had I felt so much rage for someone I didn't even know. I know they saw me, how could they not have, and they didn't even care if they hit me or not.

"What now?" Rachel asked. Matt and I were both stonily silent. "Mike, what now?" she asked again.

I looked around and grabbed the backpack. I went into the kitchen and started putting all of the food and water from the cabinets into the pack. I went to the bathroom and looked around for any medical supplies. I found band aids, Tylenol, cough medicine, pins, and thread. Back in the living room, they were both staring at me with wide eyes. My heart was racing along with the thoughts in my head. "We head out, now," I told them.

"But go where?" Matt asked.

"We go where that car was heading. Obviously, there are going to be other survivors in that direction."

"Survivors?" Rachel asked.

"That's right. As far as I know, whatever this thing is, it's killing people and it must be doing it fast, but clearly we are not the only ones left. Check for rain jackets in the closet and then let's go," I told them.

Matt went towards the bedrooms while Rachel just stood there looking at me. I looked away, not meeting her questioning eyes and she finally followed Matt. When Matt came back, he told me there were only two rain jackets in the house. "I don't need one," I replied.

"You sure, what if you get sick or something?" he asked

"I just don't care, it doesn't matter anymore."

"Hey, I know if someone tried to run me over, I would be pissed off as well, but we can't let stuff like that get to us. We have to keep our heads together." I saw Rachel come back into the room. I hitched up the other strap of the back pack on my shoulder and headed out the door.

It rained that whole night, and I felt like my head was going to explode from the built up anger that was tearing through me.

Part Two: Promises That Were Needed

When morning finally came, the rain had slowed enough to let the sun peek out. We had walked the entire night and no one spoke a word, which actually helped calm me down. We finally sat down next to sign that said Fort Worth city line. I pulled out water bottles and handed them out. "Freaking six hours on the road, and we still haven't ran into anyone. Does that sound right to any of y'all, because it sure as hell doesn't to me?" Matt said.

"Me either. How could that be?" Rachel asked me. I didn't reply right away because my eyes were fixed on a car that had flipped on the other side of the road.

They saw what I was looking at and Matt asked, "Is that the car that almost ran you over?"

"Yes, it is," I said getting up.

I grabbed the gun and cocked it. Rachel grabbed my arm then decided better of it and let go saying, "Be careful."

Examining the car, I saw there were holes on the side of it. Big ones. Peering in through the driver's side, I saw a man with cuts on his face and a large piece of glass lodged in his throat. The other seat held another man with a snapped neck. The wind blew and I felt a cold rush going through my body. I got back up and yelled, "They're dead."

But as soon as I yelled, I knew I shouldn't have. There was a terrible screeching noise behind me and I turned to see one of those things flying towards me. I fired the gun, but the bullets just ricocheted off the damn thing. I jumped out the way at the last second and the creature hit the car with full force and flopped on the ground, just like the bird back at Wal-Mart had. I scrambled back to my feet, and searched for something, anything, I could kill it with. I picked up the biggest shard of glass I could find and quickly headed towards the beast before it could regain consciousness. When I stabbed at its neck its skin was hard enough for the glass to come out of my hand and cut me. I grabbed my hand in pain. It was flopping its way towards me and I saw where it's blood was coming out. I wrapped my hand in my shirt and grabbed the glass again. I stabbed it in its wound repeatedly until it stopped moving.

Matt came behind me holding a pocket knife, "Did you kill it?" he asked.

I tried swallowing but it was hard and I said, "Yeah. Are you guys alright?"

"Don't worry about us. Jesus, your hand," he exclaimed. My hand was in a fist and when I opened it the blood started running freely.

"We have to clean that," he told me.

"I have some stuff in the pack." We headed back to other side of the road and I grabbed the water.

"You'll waste it. You need to do it slowly, let me," Rachel said grabbing the bottle.

"Fine. Matt, there is some thread in the pack it will have to be stitched up," I said.

"I'll do it. My uncle taught me some medical shit a few years ago," Rachel said. "This is not going to feel good though…" she told me apprehensively.

She slowly started pouring the water on the gash, and it felt like fire. She did it little-by-little, which made it even worse. Matt handed her the threaded needle, "Dude, there's nothing to numb it?" I shook my head, trying not to think about the pain I was already feeling.

"Matt, get him something to bite down on." He went into the pack and grabbed a towel. I took it and she told me to shove as much of the towel as I could in my mouth and bear down. Matt held my arms so I wouldn't move, and then she started stitching. The first run through with the needle felt never ending as I felt the thread slide through my skin and over the gash. I screamed into the towel with all I had in me. I could feel my eyes running over with tears. I could feel myself losing it, about to pass out, just as she knotted the end. She patted down the remaining blood and told me to drink the rest of the water. I took the towel out of my mouth and lay back waiting for the black spots in my vision to dissipate.

I drank the water slowly and smiled faintly, "Do I get a lollipop now?"

She laughed and patted my cheek. "Thank you, both of you," I told them.

Matt put his hand on my shoulder and said, "I don't think your insurance will cover the surgery." I smiled and rose up, but got really dizzy so immediately lay back down.

"Don't overdo it, Mike. You lost a good amount of blood," Rachel said, "let's just sit right here for an hour or so, ok?"

"No, we can't stay here out in the open. We could be ambushed by more of those flying shit heads." But my head and hand were killing me, so I did as she said and we sat there for about two hours before I could stand up without feeling light headed.

The weather was pretty muggy, but I still felt cold from my wet clothes. Matt was walking back and forth on the road. "Something bothering you?" Rachel asked Matt.

He stopped in his tracks, "Bothering, oh no. But there is something fucking with my head. I really want this these things killed, and I want to be there so I can piss on every one of their dead corpses for killing my...my...," he paused and took a shaky breath, "my mom."

I got up really slowly and walked up to him. "You and I have both have good reasons to hunt every one of these things down, but I remember a wise person once said that I couldn't let something get me mad, because we had to keep our heads together."

His breathing became calmer and he smirked when he said, "You gonna just throw my own words back at me?"

"I still don't know what happened to my uncle," Rachel said. I turned to her and looked around and tried to think of something to say.

"He's a strong guy," Matt said, "he's probably with other Marines kicking ass right now." She nodded her head but didn't say anything.

There was a sound approaching, and I frantically looked to see where it was coming from. In the sky, there were two jets and a black hawk coming our way. We all started yelling and jumping up and down, but all three of them passed straight over us flying towards Dallas. We grabbed our stuff hurriedly and started running after them.

We ran until we lost track of them. We were so out of breath that it felt like my lungs were going to collapse and I was starting to see black spots again. I saw Matt kick at the dirt and mumble something. I took off the backpack and put my hands over my head to get the oxygen back into my lungs.

"What now?" Matt asked, "We're not quite to the outskirts of Dallas yet, the next biggest city other than Houston."

"That might be a bad thing," Rachel said.

"Why's that?" I asked.

"Because, I think we've walked into a death trap," her voice shook. I looked where she was pointing and saw smoke coming up in the distance. I heard a thumping and the ground shook a little. There were more jets flying above us, but this time we just watched them disappear into the smoke. The thumping got more intense and I started worrying about being ambushed again, so I picked up our stuff and started walking towards the city.

"Mike, what the hell are you doing? If you haven't noticed there is something really bad going on that way," Matt said.

"I know, but those jets are going that way. Maybe they're protecting people, and there really aren't any other options. We can't go back, there's nothing to go back to." I heard their footsteps behind me.

There was a loud bang and we saw one of the jets fall out of the sky. There were more of them now. Falling from the sky in different directions, caught on fire, no tail or nose. A loud roar reached our ears, and we huddled together frozen in our fear. Matt finally pushed us towards the side of the road. We were on a bridge where a river was flowing underneath us. Looking behind us we could see two of the beast approaching us fast. They looked different than the others we had encountered though. One was skinny and had a long tail with spikes from the tip leading to its back, and the other was huge and had horns on the side of its face.

I looked over the edge of the rail again, and, quickly touching the box in my pocket, I made up my mind. "We have to jump."

Matt looked at me and looked over the edge at the thirty foot drop, "Oh, hell no! Why can't we run the other way?"

"Because those things are too close to out run now, look it's not that bad of a drop. Once we hit the water, just start swimming back under the bridge where we can take cover."

Matt started jumping up and down, which was a sign he was scared and his adrenaline was high. He opened his mouth to speak but one of those things roared and it made us cover our ears. He climbed over the edge and let out a, "Holy fuck," as he looked back at us one last time. He looked down, closed his eyes, and jumped. Rachel and I watched him fall into the river below. We waited and waited…he finally popped back up and started making his way under the bridge.

I looked and the monsters were about a football field distance away from us and coming on quick. I hopped over the rail and helped Rachel over. We looked down and Rachel held my hand. I looked into her eyes and said, "I won't let go, if you don't."

"I promise."

From then on everything slowed down. I counted to three and we both stepped off and felt the cold air rushing past us we fell. It felt like a life time. When we hit, the water it was deep, and I started kicking furiously to make my way up to the top while still grasping Rachel's hand. We reached the top and gasped for breath. The current was moving a lot faster than I expected, which made getting to the bank difficult – too difficult while holding hands and carrying a pack. I thought if I could just get Rachel to go in front of me then we'd be alright, but I couldn't get her to swing around. The current seemed to be getting faster. We started kicking harder and we were getting closer. I saw a tree limb hanging over the river and I paddled with my one hand to grab it. Pulling up on the limb, I could hear it starting to break apart. I pulled Rachel as hard as I could through the current so she could reach the bank, and she did the same for me right before the limb broke off completely.

We laid there breathing heavily for a moment, and I started laughing. I looked at Rachel and she too was smiling. "This should be a new event at the Olympics or something," she said.

I let out a chuckle and sat up, and looked down the river and saw where rocks were sticking out not far from where we got out.

"Dodged a bullet there. Heh, wasn't that hard for you was it, Matt?" I waited for an answer, but was faced with only silence. I looked around and called out his name again, but no answer. I got up quick, which made me a little dizzy, and I yelled out his name.

"This isn't funny, man," I could feel my heart sink, "MATT!"

Rachel was frantically searching the bank, and then it occurred to me that he never got out of the water. I started running down the bank of the river, looking over the rocks for any sign of him. I stepped on something slippery, and looked down to notice fresh blood that led into the woods. My eyes widened at the thought of those fuckers carrying him off somewhere. I started following the trail and the more I followed it the more it seemed like he was losing a lot of blood. The blood came to a stop with a dead deer. I was relieved all of the blood wasn't Matt's, but he still was nowhere in sight.

I tried yelling out his name again, but there was still no response. I heard Rachel coming up behind me as I took off the backpack and hunched over to catch my breath. "He's somewhere, we just have to keep looking," she said.

"We can't its getting dark. We could walk around these woods all night and only get lost ourselves," I told her.

"Well, I'm not staying near that thing. For sure, it will attract the monsters," she pointed to the deer.

I got up and picked up the backpack and looked inside. There was a hole in the bottom and nothing left inside. It must have torn on one of the rocks in the river. I threw it to the ground. I was in a rage and punched a tree with my bad hand not caring about the pain. I looked up and yelled, "My mom, my dad, and now my best friend. What else? Why us? What the hell do you want from us?"

I took a deep breath and licked my lips, "We go that way," I pointed the way the river was flowing, "I saw it curve down going back towards the city. He must have been carried downstream."

Rachel was looking at my hand and she took out a pocket knife and cut a piece from her shirt. She wrapped my hand tightly with the strip and smiled crookedly. "Thanks," I said blandly.

I wish I could've smiled, but at that time I just couldn't muster one.

"Lead the way," she told me. We walked, all the while searching for any sign of Matt, until I found a spot under some trees. Rachel sat down and looked up staring into the trees above.

"What are you looking at?"

"The bodies."

I looked up and stunned to see bodies that were caught in the trees some hanging upside down with their legs dangled in the branches. They must have been some of the pilots of the jets that were struck down. I blinked and looked away. Quietly, we moved on to another location.

We sat down in a safe location, still not having seen any sign from Matt. Rachel lay down and I told her I would watch for the rest of the night. Before shutting her eyes, she turned to me and said, "He's fine I just know it."

As I stayed up, I listened to the sounds that filled the night. It was a calm night and the running water was peaceful, but I still felt frightened. I finally, without waking Rachel, laid down and fell asleep.

When I woke up the sun was in the sky, but there were no birds chirping. I sat up and dusted off the dirt from my clothes. I looked to my side to wake up Rachel, but she wasn't there. I immediately started to freak out. I got to my feet and ran towards to the river. I yelled out her name and she quickly replied behind me. I turned around and flung my arms around her.

"I thought something bad happened to you. Where did you go?"

"I had to take a shit."

I looked at her and we both laughed. After a somewhat decent night's sleep, we started walking again this time talking to ease our pain almost like we were sitting on top of my roof again with our only cares being an upcoming test. It was almost like a nostalgic feeling.

"Were you talking to God yesterday?" she asked me.

"What do you mean?" I replied.

"God, were you angry with him?"

"I guess. I mean, my mom and my dad are dead, we're lost, we have no food, who knows what has happened to Matt, I can't tell if I'm being fucked with or if I'm dead and this is hell."

"So you blame God?"

"Well, someone created those monsters."

"Maybe…maybe this was supposed to happen?"

"I don't want to think about it that way."

"Why not, what if this is God's calling or something?"

"Rachel, just stop with the bullshit!" I exclaimed. She was starting to sound like that guy on the radio and it was scaring me. She looked down. I took a deep breath in, "I'm sorry, it's just if I wanted to be preached to I would've gone to church more often."

She chuckled then said, "I'm sorry, too. I was starting to sound like my grandmother. When I went to live with my uncle, he didn't take me to church as much when I stayed with my grandparents. And I guess, I've had a lot to think about since all that happened."

I grabbed my pocket and felt the box. I thought about giving it to her right then, but decided not to. What we were going through, our lives right now, was bigger than just us. We had stopped walking when the conversation got heated, and I was suddenly able to hear sticks breaking behind us. My eyes widened and I headed towards the sounds. I had a smile on my face, just knowing it was Matt, but, before I could call out Matt's name, I came upon two of the monsters feasting on a raccoon and possum.

My smile was gone instantly and I felt Rachel behind me. I was pushing her to back up quietly, but as I did the birds were startled and fluttered up. The things heads snapped up and looked at us and made that piercing noise. "Run!" I yelled at Rachel as she was already heading back to the river bank.

One of the monsters cut us off and the other closed in behind us. I looked at Rachel and gave her a sign to get ready to drop. She understood and we waited for them to attack. Soon enough one of them pointed their tail at us and charged. I waited until the last second and pulled her down. It unintentionally stabbed its comrade which then started convulsing violently.

While the other was still confused, we started running. It wasn't long before we heard the creature approaching us. I stopped and pushed Rachel behind me to protect her. I braced myself for what was coming, not knowing what else to do, but suddenly the creature's tail was sliced off. It fell on the ground writhing in pain as an axe came down hard on its head. Our rescuer turned around, and we ran to Matt as we realized it was him.

He took a deep breath in and said, "Hey, guys." When I finished hugging him, Rachel jumped up and kissed him quick on the cheek.

"Where the hell were you, we looked all over for you? You had poor Michael all sick and worried."

"Yeah, sorry about that. I'll tell you all about it, but right now follow me I gotta show y'all something."

Telling Matt now about the night we spent without him, all he could do was laugh. He kept saying the look on our faces when we figured out who was wielding the axe was priceless. He made a face that was over exaggerating. I can't believe that was over a year ago and still shit's in the fire.

That day when Matt found us, he told us how he couldn't force his self to get to the side and said he drifted for about two miles downstream just exhausted. When he saw someone near the bank, he yelled to get his attention which he successfully did. By then, he was out of breath and dizzy from yelling and thrashing around so much. The man that helped him out of the water was, of all people, Mr. Stooping. After Matt rested for a few hours, he started walking back up stream to find us, which is when he killed the monster and saved us.

Coming up on the spot where Matt made it out of the river, we saw Mr. Stooping fishing. I was really happy and relieved to see a familiar face. He looked over with a cheek-to-cheek smile. He set down the fishing pole down and came over and hugged Rachel and me.

"So glad to see both of you in one piece," he said.

"You too, Mr. Stooping."

"No need to call me mister anymore. Just call me Mark."

"Gotcha."

"So sorry to hear about your folks, if you ever want to talk, I'm here for yuh. And also for the rest of y'all," he said, eyeing Rachel and Matt.

My heart felt comforted, but then I realized something, "Where's Mrs. Stooping?"

He sighed and wiped his forehead, "She's no longer with us or little Shelia."

"I'm so sorry to hear that," Rachel told him.

He gave a little chuckle, "I'll be fine, she's up there with the Big Man, probably nagging him right now."

We all smiled and Matt said, "God, even in the afterlife I might deal with women still being bitchy?"

"Stay young while you still can, son. The female race will be here for quite a while."

Matt made his fingers into gun and pretended to shoot his brains out and Mark gave him a thumbs up. We all had a much needed laugh, and the whole time I felt like everything was normal even if just for that few minutes. But the truth of it all caught up to me soon enough when I realized we still have no shelter or food.

Mark and his wife were heading north just like we were, hoping for an area guarded by the military where they would be protected. They made it all the way to Waco before they encountered any of the monsters. They had been following a bunch of other cars, but when the creatures turned up people panicked. That's when he crashed into another car going way too fast. When Mrs. Stooping's airbag didn't deploy he knew she wasn't going to make it out alive. When he opened the door to crawl out, Shelia, scared from the crash, jumped out and was hit by a car and killed instantly. He found another car and drove that one until it ran out of gas. From there, he walked until he saw the river. He had been camping near the river for two days when he heard Matt calling for help.

His story was just as sad as our own, but I was overjoyed that he found us when he did. While he was in the second car, he heard on the radio that the same attacks were happening all over the world – China, Turkey, New Zealand and so many others. His voice shook when he said the pyramids had come down by those things. It made me shiver, as if it was snowing – which I'm glad it wasn't. Rachel asked if there were any other attacks around the U.S. There were. Miami was hit not long after Texas, but San Francisco and California in general has had it the worst from what he heard.

"Are there any safe areas we could go?" I asked, "We were thinking of heading further into Dallas before we got cut off."

"That's exactly where I was going to head last night, but I saw Matthew drifting down the river, plans changed a bit. Since y'all are all here now, I think we should sleep here for another night and get started in the morning."

"As much I would love to sleep under the stars and be killed in my sleep, I think we should try going a little further towards the city and finding a more suitable place to sleep. Perhaps something with a bed..." Matt said.

"I agree with that idea," Rachel said.

Mark licked his lips and thought about it. Then he looked at the sun which was high in the sky. He finally said, "Okay, there's a way to the city that's not on the main road about a mile that way," he said as he pointed in the direction of the current, "then it's about a good twenty miles to downtown, but we might find people and food on the outskirts."

We all got up to our feet and Mark led the way. I was behind everyone else and thought that we might just be safe now. With Mark being a professional doctor and an adult, he would know a little bit more about how to survive, and honestly I was ready to let someone else be the leader of our group.

Matt was still carrying the axe and I asked him where he had got it. He told me it was just stuck in a tree stump. I thought about the person that might have been using it, some kind of lumberjack I guess.

We reached a ladder that someone had built where the bank was too steep to walk up. We climbed up it one-by-one, but my hand started hurting from having to grip the rungs. When I reached the top I looked at the stitches and they were still holding on tight. Mark asked if I was alright and asked what happened.

"We had to stitch his hand from a glass cut," Rachel said.

"Let me see it." He squinted at my hand, turned it over, and then back again. "Who stitched this?"

"I did, sir," Rachel told him with a nervous voice.

He smiled and told her she did a great job and asked where she learned to stitch like that. "My uncle did."

"I figured he was the one. Most military men have seen many injuries and learn how to treat them effectively in the field. Your uncle is a great man he is probably protecting our country at this very minute and worrying about you all at the same time." She smiled faintly, and Mark went to hug her tightly.

We walked all afternoon at a pretty good pace until there was a stench strong enough to remind me of the bodies back at the gas station. Our guard was up so we slowed down and listened carefully. When we reached the top of the next hill we could see smoke rising in the distance. The tall buildings of downtown Dallas were smoking and the smell of death was encompassing. At that point, I knew it was a bad sign, but we continued anyways.

When we reached the outskirts of the city, all of the stores appeared to have been broken into and the streets were riddled with burning trash and junk. Mark yelled out, "Hello?" but like always there was no reply. We walked deeper into the city and I kept hearing something but just a faint something. It sounded like...talking. It grew stronger, and I was getting anxious. It was coming from a store so I went ahead of everyone, stepping over the broken window glass and made my way to an overturned desk. Under a pile of papers and books was a military two-way radio.

There was a man on the other end calling out for anyone to answer. I picked it up and held down the mic button and said, "Hello, hello? I'm here!"

I waited and the man replied back and asked who I was, "My name is Michael Thompson, I am here with Rachel Marie, and Matthew Jones, and Mark Stooping all from the Houston area."

I waited and there was a long pause until finally he replied back, "Michael? This is Jeff, Rachel's uncle."

"Hello, Michael you still there?"

When I went to reply, Rachel snatched the radio from me, "Uncle Jeff? Where are you? We're in some kind of electronic store." Her voice was wavering and I could tell she was trying not to cry.

"Hunny, I need you to calm down. Our station is about six miles from your position. Head north. In three blocks take a left, and then go another two blocks and wait for me there. We'll walk the rest of the way together."

"Okay, okay we can do that."

"Be careful, I need you to leave the radio there, in case some other civilians find it."

"I love you."

"Just be careful, and stick to the buildings."

We walked out of the store and headed north. Rachel was walking faster than all of us. She was basically jogging. When we came to the third block and made a left, Rachel just gave up all pretenses and started running. We told her to slow down, but before we knew it we came to the second block. She was looking around frantically, and suddenly yelled out, "JEFF" at the top of her lungs. Her cry echoed throughout the empty buildings and then we all stood in silence waiting willing him to reply.

"Rachel! Rachel!" Jeff came hurdling around the corner and scooped up his niece in a bear hug. Rachel burst into tears, and it took several minutes for her to calm down.

"Is everyone alright?" Jeff asked still holding onto Rachel. We all nodded and he smiled. He looked at his niece and wiped away her tears and told her, "Let's get you all somewhere safe." We all smiled and followed him.

"Dr. Stooping?" Jeff called out.

"Call me Mark, sir." he replied.

"Mark, how did you know to come here?"

"Radio. Kept saying to go north. I got as far as the car took me."

"And your wife, where is she?"

He cleared his throat, "Dead, sir."

Jeff let out a breath of air, "So sorry for you. I offer my condolences to you, sir."

"Thank you. Really appreciate it."

"What about you Michael?"

"My parents are dead as well. Car crashed. My dad didn't have his seat belt on I guess. But, before that we heard to go north on the radio, too."

He stopped and looked at me, really looked at me. He looked at me as if he were seeing the horrors I had seen. "They were great people, and they raised a swell young man. Is it the same for you, Matthew." He looked over at Matt and he nodded. Jeff looked up and whispered, "Jesus, why the hell is this happening?"

"Mike has been our sort of captain getting us here. We just ran into Mark earlier today," Rachel said.

Jeff looked at her then said to me earnestly, "Well, son, thank you for keeping Rachel safe for me."

"You're welcome. It was an honor," I told him and we continued on walking.

We made it to the base, which looked like an overgrown campsite. There were mostly small tents, but then one large tent. I asked how many people were here and he replied that there weren't that many anymore. He told us that many of the people who made it here were already dead or dying. There were over a hundred people, but now the camp held about ten. The people that came here had missing limbs, viruses, or were bleeding internally.

"We tried saving as many as we could, but we had little staff to care for that many people and even more injuries." We came up to the largest tent, and he held the flap open as we entered. There were a bunch of televisions and computers with maps on the screens. There were little red dots on one of the screens and a huge black area on others. I was too scared to ask what they meant, but that didn't stop Matt from asking.

There was a man that quickly said, "It's government business," but Jeff told him not to worry and turned to us.

"The red dots represent where the monsters first originated. Most of it happened in Russia, the Czech Republic, and Madagascar. The ones here in America are Colorado, New Mexico, and Georgia."

"And the black areas?" Mark asked.

Jeff rubbed his head, "Those represent the areas that we assume to be completely wiped out."

This made it very hard to swallow. My eyes widened and hoped someone would ask to clarify what he had just said. No one did so I took a deep breath of courage and asked, "What do you mean wiped out? Like no survivors?" Jeff nodded, casting his eyes down. I could see clearly the deep, black circles that encased his eyes.

The black areas were wide places like Germany and Nigeria and Korea. There were many others, but I kept myself from looking at the screen any further.

"Now wait a minute," Mark said, waving his hand like there was a fly bothering him, "this all happened in a course of a few days? How are you so certain that a whole country as big as Germany could be taken out?"

Another man that was sitting next to a computer said, "There were more than 15 of those things in every major city. We speculate that the population that weren't in a big city, either evacuated or offed themselves."

"Jake, calm down. You don't need to fill their brains with this," another man with a hat said.

"Why the hell NOT!" the man roared. "The more we try to kill those things, the more casualties we get. We can't run from the truth of that. I'm getting sick and tired of losing more and more people, many of which I consider friends and family."

"Has anyone killed one of the big ones yet?" Rachel asked.

"Just the little fuckers. They're more of parasites than what the big ones are."

"Parasites? You mean like leeches or something?"

"You can think of it like that," the man with the hat said. "We saw one of the bigger ones that had a smaller one attached to it. When the little one fell off they unravel their selves like they were in a cocoon. They resemble what could be like a crab or a scorpion." I hope he meant there were only the ones that looked like the scorpions. I don't want to come across a crab-like one. He continued, "They have tails that point out to strike when they attack. When you are hit with it, it's like your body is exposed to acid and your skin starts to peel off with a terrible burning sensation. Then, your eyes will start to roll to the back of your head and you convulse until your body shuts down. This all takes around six to eight minutes."

"You've seen it happen, sir?" Mark asked.

"I didn't, Lieutenant Jeff did."

"That's all for now, Robbie. Keep an eye out for activity," Jeff said.

"But, sir-"

"NOW, don't let me repeat myself. Do I make myself clear?" Jeff bellowed.

"Yes, sir," Robbie said as he went back to monitoring the screen.

I could only hear fear and anger in Jeff's voice, and I knew he experienced something that he could never forget. He showed us out and led us to another, smaller tent. There were two blow-up mattresses on the ground. He told Matt and I to share this tent; Mark would have another. Rachel was going to share her uncle's tent.

Meeting back near the main tent, he took us to meet an older lady that was stirring something in a big pot. "Miss Susan, what delicious meal are you preparing for us tonight?" Jeff asked the lady.

"Chicken, sir. It'll be ready by sundown." She looked over and stopped what she was doing and smiled, "Newcomers?"

"This young lady is my niece, Rachel, and two of her friends, Michael and Matthew. This gentleman is Mark Stooping a former doctor from the same city I was last stationed in."

She moved her fading blonde hair to the side and gave us a howdy, "Doctor, huh, what area did you work in?"

"I worked in a critical care unit."

"So, you know what to do if someone loses a limb or something in that nature?"

"I think I could manage, yes ma'am."

She smiled and turned her attention on Matt, Rachel, and me, "You kids must be starving, huh?" We all nodded. "Well, don't y'all worry one bit, I'll have a decent meal ready in about two hours or so." We couldn't wait to finally eat something that wasn't candy or from a can.

We walked back to our tents to get situated and rest for a bit. Matt and I just lay in our beds and listened to the silence. Before I knew it, Matt was snoring, but I held my laughter in so I wouldn't wake him. I didn't blame him for being so tired, all that shit that happened earlier today and yesterday must have exhausted him. The only thing that was making a sound – besides Matt – was the wind. Soon enough, I heard thunder in the distance and started to get anxious. Before I could completely freak out, there were footsteps approaching and Jeff opened the flap to the tent asking me to follow him.

We went out past the other tents and he looked at me with a smile, "I just want to thank you again for keeping my niece safe." I told him it was no problem and he held up his hand, "You were always a great friend to her and to see you both pull yourselves together through a crisis like this, really shows your bravery."

He reached to the side of his hip, "I want you to have my nine millimeter. Rachel said you were pretty good with a handgun." I took it from him not knowing how to respond. "We'll be moving out of here in a few days. Orders came in from a higher authority. When we do, I'll have a backpack with gear ready for you."

I wanted to thank him, but all I could think about was who the higher authority could be? Why did we have to move if we're in a secure spot? But, I shook off the questions long enough to thank him. He walked me back to my tent and told me that if I or Matt needed something to give him a holler.

Matt was still snoring and I sat on my bed and studied the weapon in my hands. I checked to see if it was loaded, which it was. I kept playing his words in my head, about Rachel and me staying together during a time like this. I had thought before about what I would do if she wasn't with me in this. *Would I still be as brave, if I didn't have her to be brave for?* Then I remembered the ring in my pocket. I took it out and looked at it. The inside of the box was still a little damp, but the onside was as dry as lips in a desert. I stared at the ring, trying to recreate that whole night with the ending I had been hoping for. Giving her the box, seeing her open it, and then…I couldn't finish it. No matter how I imagined it, it came out blank. I closed the box and put it back in my pocket. I lay back down and stared at the piece of wood that was holding up the tent. My mind was buzzing with questions. *Higher authority? Where are we moving to exactly? What makes that a safer place than here? What happens if Texas gets wiped out?* I fell asleep in the sea of questions storming in my mind.

I had a dream that a forest was on fire and I was following a child. The child kept yelling for his mother wondering around aimlessly. The fire was turning into a dark red mass that was taking shape, but I couldn't yell out to him to run. Suddenly, the child stopped where he was and looked to me; he pointed behind me and screamed. I turned to find myself in the shadow of a creature so huge I never had time to identify it before it's jaws clamped down over me. I jumped awake to find Matt looking over me.

"Was I snoring loud?" I asked.

"No, but you were talking in your sleep," he said.

"Really, what did I say?"

"Something like 'Come back, hey, I'm right here.' You alright, you seem pretty stressed?"

"Well, shouldn't you be too since there is a giant Cloverfield, Godzilla-like thing destroying our world."

"Yeah, of course, but on the bright side of things, there isn't any homework to turn in and at least we are with Jeff and the military now."

I sat up and peered out the tent flap to see it was already dark. There were rain clouds making their way towards us bringing the thunder and lightning ever closer. I looked for my gun and found it under the sheets as I told Matt about moving to another area and Jeff giving me the gun.

"Well, I don't want to stay here like sitting ducks," Matt told me, "and if you didn't notice it seems like Jeff is in charge. He is a lieutenant, but there are other ranks in the military."

"I guess you're right. I guess the way he said 'higher authority' made it sound weird."

"How did it sound?"

"Like…I don't know…there was a weird pause and the way he looked around. It caught me off guard, really."

"So, you think there's some kind of conspiracy going on here?"

"No, I don't know. Maybe I'm just over analyzing things."

He looked at me and it looked like he was searching for a way to amke smile but said, "I get that we are going through some serious apocalypse kind of shit right now that doesn't make a whole lot of since, but just be careful on what you look into is all."

He got up and started pushing me outside, "Come on I'm starving."

Just outside, Rachel had been coming over to get us for dinner, so we walked to the large tent together. There were plates lined up with equal portions of chicken, red beans, and a slice of bread. Everyone grabbed a plate and sat down on folded chairs that had been set up for the meal.

This was the first time that we would be able to see the other people living at the camp. I noticed there was an Asian brother and sister, an old white man with an even older style mustache, a man that looked like an oversized Morgan Freeman, and a young couple and their Boston terrier.

We ate our food mostly in silence until Jeff spoke up, "I received information that we can no longer remain in this spot, as such we'll be heading north. Most likely Tennessee." No one made a comment, so Jeff continued, "A bus will arrive around 0600 the day after tomorrow. We need to be ready by that time."

The young Asian guy held up his hand. "You're not in school son, you can speak up," Jeff told him.

"Right, when is 0600?"

"It's six in the morning," the man with the mustache replied

"Oh, ok…thanks."

"Mm hmm."

"Why do we have to move?" The Asian sister asked, "Aren't we safe here?"

"In God's honesty, no. And we might not be safe until this whole mess is cleared up. Until then, we need to rally together with other survivors."

"Why? Won't that attract the monsters?" the overweight Morgan Freeman asked.

"The more people we have the more people who can be trained to use military weapons to fight," Jake said.

"Plus," Robbie interjected, "there's a better chance of having more people around with medical knowledge to assist with injuries. There will also be a higher chance of being better protected."

Everyone was quiet again and there was a clash of thunder. We all cleared our plates and threw them away in a plastic bag. Jeff told us to stay in our tents the whole night, "If you need to go to the restroom do it by your tent. Do not wander off."

Matt and I went into our tents. Matt took off his shirt and crawled into bed; I put my gun by the side of my bed and followed suit. The wind was starting to increase and it made the tent feel even less secure. The rain started, but I was too exhausted to have the energy to worry about the storm.

I woke up and had the urge to take a piss. The rain was coming down pretty hard, but I just couldn't hold it in. I put my shoes on and walked out. I went to the side of the tent, unzipped my pants and proceeded to pee. When I finished, I heard someone walking on the other side of the tent. I looked and saw the Asian brother heading towards the forest. I went inside my tent and grabbed my gun. I walked past their tent and heard his sister sleeping still. I looked around, but I couldn't see where he went. I walked cautiously in the direction of the forest. I didn't want to call for him, but didn't want to leave him out there alone either.

I was about to turn back until I heard a crunching noise. I cocked my gun, but it was still by my hip. The noise was coming closer, and then I was able to see the brother making his way back. He looked at me and immediately got mad.

"What are you doing? Were you spying on me, pervert?"

"Lieutenant Jeff said to stay by our tents and not to go far. No matter what."

"I had to take a shit. What you want me to stink up the camp?"

"Better than getting yourself killed and attracting those things to the camp."

He looked at my gun and began to laugh loudly, "Were you going to kill me? Is that it? Make room for less people to protect? You sorry SONOFABITCH!" I started to backup when he started walking towards me. "I have a sister! Were you going to kill her too."

"I wasn't going to kill anyone. It's just for protection. Lower your voice a little you might attract-"

"I don't believe you. No, what if I kill you? Huh, how does that sound?" he said, cutting me off. He put up his hands up like he was getting ready to fight me, so I stepped back even more and raised my hands up to show him I didn't want to fight.

"I'LL KILL YO-" he yelled out just as a spike went through the back of his head leaving his left eye dangling. The spiked end of one of the flying monsters tails slid out of his head, and he dropped lifelessly to the ground. The creature was momentarily occupied with its fresh kill, so I snuck back towards camp as quietly as I could.

In Jeff's tent, I woke him up hurriedly spilling out what had just happened. He looked at me like I was a little kid who had just woken up from a nightmare. "Are you sure?" he asked in a low, deep voice.

"He was stabbed in the head. I saw it," I told him now getting his full attention. He put on his boots and followed me after grabbing his gun from under his mattress. We came to the body which now was a headless body and the back of his insides were showing. He looked forward as if the things were watching us. Then he looked at me. I could only think, *Where's the monster? Do they only eat the heads or something?*

"Who was he?"

"The Asian brother. He kept yelling and I tried to calm him down but it was too late."

"What was he yelling about?"

"Sir, I don't think we should be talking right here. What if those things come back?"

I heard him swallow and he blinked really fast, he finally said, "Alright let's head back."

When we walked back I kept getting the feeling we were being watched. We reached the camp and Jeff stopped and said, "When it's morning, I'll tell the Ms. Dia about her brother, but until then I want you to go back to bed. Got it?"

I was about to respond when I saw one of those things charging at us. Before I could alert Jeff, the bastard impaled him in the back. He looked up to see the monster, and then pushed himself off the spiked tail. He fell on the ground, and as he did he flipped around and quickly shot the monster in the mouth before it bit him. The creature died almost instantly.

I pulled Jeff out from underneath the dead monster, and saw him shivering. I called out help several times, but knew there was nothing anyone could do. He coughed up a great amount of blood and in a weak voice he said, "You did a great job at it before," he coughed a little more in between the convulsions, "please, take care of my niece. Protect her." I looked at him, my eyes filled with tears, and I nodded my head.

I could hear others starting to come up around us, but Rachel's screams drowned them out. She threw herself on Jeff looking for a way to stop the bleeding. He grabbed her hands to still them, "I'm sorry. I love you," he said.

Rachel looked at him and through her tears said, "I will always love you." He smiled and then shut his eyes for the last time. Rachel continued to hold him, sobs wracking her thin body. The rain was beginning to slow, but my face was still drenched in my own tears.

I looked around and everyone was crowded around. The sister was searching around for her brother. I got up and went over to her. I cleared my throat and said, "Ms. Dia," she looked at me with panic in her eyes. I wanted to say that her brother was dead and it was his fault that Jeff died too, but instead I told her, "Your brother is dead. He went out into the woods and he died there by one of the monsters. I'm sorry." Her eyes filled with tears and she ran back to her tent. I felt bad for her, that her brother was stupid enough to leave camp and consider himself immune to the dangers that now inhabited our world.

I looked back at Rachel; she was still holding her uncle. I went back and kneeled beside her. I coaxed her arms off the corpse of her uncle, and, as if she was waiting for me, she turned automatically into my embrace. We stayed like that, not caring for the others, I let her cry until she was ready to stop only hugging her tighter.

As the rain died down completely, so did Rachel's tears. The sun was beginning to rise, and I suggested for her to go back to her tent and rest for a bit. She looked at me and said, "Will you come with me?"

"Yes, but you go ahead I have to talk with Robbie and Jake." I helped her up and she headed back to her tent.

I walked over to Robbie and Jake and looked at them, "We need to leave here as soon as possible."

"We can't," Robbie began. "The orders were to wait another day until the bus arrives."

"Oh, fuck that," Jake exclaimed. "Look at what just happened. You seriously think that these people will want to stay here any longer?"

"Do you want to get it from the general?"

"I'd rather hear him scream his lungs out than die here."

"What if we can meet the bus on the road? It should be coming from the north right?" I asked.

"I like his idea. We round up everything we absolutely need and head out. ASAP." Jake said.

Robbie looked at both of us and said, "Fine. Just give me a few hours to contact the base and see if they can get the bus to leave out any earlier."

"Just figure out the bus, and I'll start getting packed up," I told them.

I walked back to Rachel's tent and saw she was balled up with no covers on. I put the covers over her and sat on Jeff's bed. "Are we going to be alright? What are we supposed to do now?" she pleaded.

"I will do whatever I can to protect you," I paused and then said, "I promise." She looked at me as if seeing me for the first time. She sat up and came over to Jeff's bed. She reached for my face and then we were kissing. Her lips were soft and it made my heart pound, and in that moment it felt like we were all each other had.

She held my face in her hands, looking at me intensely, "I don't want you to leave my life," she said.

"Don't leave mine either," I told her.

"I promise," she said.

She fell asleep in my arms, but I quietly carried her to her own bed. Looking down on her sleeping, I said, "I have something for you. I've held onto it and wanted to give it to you for a while now…but it has just never been the right time…and I don't think this is it either." She was still asleep and all I could was hope that that moment would come soon. I grabbed a bag, one I assume used to be Jeff's, and started packing up supplies that he had laying around.

I had been working for a while, when to Robbie walked into the tent and said, "We just got news from base, and we are cleared to leave immediately."

I tried to shush him, but it was too late. Rachel rolled over and said, "Wait, what's happening?"

"We're getting out of here," I said. She got up and helped me finish the rest of the packing, adding her own bag to the mix.

When we finished packing, we walked out and I looked over to where Jeff's body was supposed to be, but it was nowhere in sight. I glanced around discreetly, not wanting to alarm Rachel to its absence, to see if it was placed somewhere else, but I continued to the larger tent. Jake was standing outside and told me that most everyone was ready to go. I asked him what happened to Jeff's body.

"You're best friend took him and buried him," he said.

"Matt? Why him?"

"He said he was an honorable man that deserved to be buried."

"Where is he buried?" Rachel asked coming from behind me. Jake pointed behind the large tent, and Rachel started walking in that direction.

"How is the sister? The one that lost her brother," I asked Jake.

"She's dead, slit her wrist in her tent." I let out a sigh, but I couldn't say I was surprised.

"When do we leave?"

"Less than an hour," he said. I nodded and went to see how Rachel was doing. She was standing next to a pile of rocks with a sunflower on top of it. When I walked up next to her, she grabbed my hand.

"I'm sorry. I wanted to give him a manlier flower but this is all I could find," Matt said from behind us.

Rachel turned and hugged him saying, "Thank you. This means a lot to me."

"No problem. No really, the thank you was fine, the hugging is a little awkward," he said and she laughed.

We all stood there looking down at the sunflower, until Rachel placing her hand on top of the flower said, "I love you, Uncle Jeff."

We helped Robbie pack up the last of the equipment in the large tent, and then Jake announced that it was time to head out. Gathered around, everybody was carrying a pack, if not two, looking sullen and anxious all at the same time.

"Um," the man with the long mustache started, "I think I'm going to head back to my own city and wait things out there. Don't worry; I can make it on my own."

"Are you sure you want to do this," Robbie asked him.

"Yeah, been thinking about this all day, it's where I belong."

Jake walked up to him and handed him a gun with a few bullets, "Make them last."

"Thank you, sir," he said taking them and turning to head off alone.

"Now, is everybody else heading north towards the bus and Tennessee?" Jake asked. Everyone looked around and the man that looked like a big Morgan Freeman raised his hand. Jake didn't even wait to hear where he was going, just handed him another gun and a few bullets and told him the same thing. Everyone else stood still.

"Ok then, we walk until we're on the border of Texas. Then, we stop there and have us a little supper. After that we keep walking until we meet the bus," Jake told us, "Agreed?"

We all agreed. Shouldering our packs, Robbie came up to me with a small backpack and quietly told me Lieutenant Jeff wanted me to have it. I took it and looked inside. There was a gun with extra bullets, a compass, a map of the United States, and batteries. There was also a note, but I waited to read it.

Jake told the remainder of us to stay as close together as possible, and with that last bit of advice we headed towards the road. Robbie had a radio on the back of his pack and he was holding the mic, like he was hoping he would hear someone announce the Spurs had won against the Heat. Jake was always looking around. There were times that I thought he would get whip lash from turning his head so much. The young couple held hands and the woman held her dog. Miss Susan was carrying her pack with pans hanging off the side. Matt had made sure to carry his axe and was walking with Mark. I looked at Rachel, taking her hand, and she gave me a small smile.

Three hours passed and the young couple was starting to fall behind. Jake saw this and yelled out for them to keep up. They were sweating pretty badly and Miss. Susan asked if we could take a small water break. Jake quickly said no, but Robbie talked him into taking a small ten minute break. We dropped our packs like they were weighted down with bricks and plopped down next to them.

Robbie was messing with his radio, when Jake asked, "Did you hear that?"

"Hear what?" he replied

Robbie messed with it a little more and there was a slight static of a voice, "That. Did you hear that?"

Jake now had a concerned look on his face, "Go back a few channels. Right...there!"

We all listened to the faint voice, but all that could be made out was "Go- I repeat- It- Dammit Rob, get a...clear channel?"

He turned the knob on the radio slowly and we heard a man clearly, "Go back, the creature is on your path, take shelter. I REPEAT - It is heading your way. Code 6991 is now affirmative."

"What does that mean, that code?" Miss Susan asked.

"It's a new code. I'm not sure what it means, but whatever it is I'm damn sure I don't want to be on this road right now," Robbie said.

Trembles were starting to make their way through to us, and we all grabbed our packs and ran as best we could to get off the road. The trembles were coming faster and faster and young couple's dog began to bark. Jake kept yelling to shut that mutt up, but the dog was losing it and jumped out of the woman's arms. It ran the opposite direction we were heading and the woman started yelling for it while the her husband held her back. Then the trembles stopped. We were all quiet; the only sounds the bark of the Boston terrier now fading away.

"Is the road...cracking?" Robbie asked looking at Jake. The trembles came back stronger than ever as a monster broke its way free from the ground right where Jake and Robbie were standing. They were instantly swallowed into the mouth of the snake like monster. The breaking ground sent the rest of us scattering in random directions. The young couple ran the way of their dog, Miss Susan went to the left with Mark, and Matt, Rachel, and I ran to the right. The monster was like a giant snake with the legs of a millipede that slithered its way after the young couple. We hid in a ditch and watched as the monster caught up to them, rose its body up, and then dove into the ground like it was a pool, taking the helpless couple down with it. The ground stilled and I searched for Mark and Miss Susan without any luck, but I did see the small ring box. I felt my pocket and noticed there was a rip.

Before I could second guess myself, I ran to grab the box with Matt and Rachel yelling at me to stop. I reached the box and stored it safely in my backpack. I looked up to hear Mark's running feet. He had blood on his shirt face and yelled, "Go back."

"But where is Miss Susan?"

"Dead. She's dead. The little ones got her," he said passing me by.

Back in the ditch I said, "We have to keep going north."

"The bus is probably not even coming anymore," Mark said.

"I know, but we do know there is nothing to go back to. Moving forward is the only option." I had their attention. "We keep going and hopefully the bus picks up. The border to Oklahoma is not that far. After that, we head a little more north then east to Tennessee." They all agreed, but we made a long detour around the last strike location before we got back to the road.

We reached the border of Texas by the time it was dark. We were all exhausted, thirsty, and hungry. We thought if we would walk a little further we might find someone or something to provide food or shelter, so we just kept going…and going.

I started to develop a slight cough that eventually turned into a full blown cold. Mark noticed and made us stop so he could take a look at me. He felt my head and said that I felt warm and that my throat was swollen. I told him I was fine and that we had to keep going, but he disagreed.

"No, you might get even sicker and that might lead to pneumonia. There's a small town up ahead. We should look for a pharmacy," he said.

We reached the town and spied a Walgreen's not too far away. The doors to the store were locked, but Matt and Mark started kicking at the door. At told them to move away as I pulled out my gun and shot straight at the glass. It made a hole, so I started beating it with the butt of my gun to widen it. The glass finally broke apart and we entered the store. It was dark and it seemed like nothing had been touched, surprisingly. We walked in silence following Mark down the cold medicine aisle.

"This might make you drowsy, but you should start feeling better in a few days," he said pouring it into the little cup. He handed it to me and I gulped it down, my face twitched a little from the taste of it.

"I hate grape flavored medicine," I said. Mark only laughed.

Since the town was still fairly intact we decided to only take a few supplies for the night and find some place to stay close. That way, we could come back in the morning to stock up.

We all headed back outside and walked to a traffic light that was blinking red, yellow, and green. We made a decision to perhaps find a motel instead of breaking into someone's house. We walked a little further and found a Holiday Inn. The lobby looked trashed and the music was still playing, it made me shiver to hear the eerily calm almost happy tunes. Matt and I went behind the counter to find the card keys.

"One room?" I yelled out.

"No, two will do," Mark hollered back.

I took two key cards out and handed them to Matt, who took them and turned on the computer.

"Maybe you should go check out the gift shop...ya' know see if there is any food and shit," Matt said.

"Okay, we'll go look for food for us and shit for you," Rachel said.

It was great to see she still had some sense of humor after what happened the other night. Rachel and I went to the gift shop and saw that it too was trashed. There was no food or drinks, but there were clothes. She went through them and picked out a t-shirt. I told her to get several and I would put them in my backpack. I picked out a few shirts for me and Matt. I picked up a hat and put it on Rachel. We laughed and she said she would keep it.

"Do you think Mark would like this?" Rachel asked me. I turned around to see her holding up a button down, green shirt. I gave her a thumbs up, and we headed back to find Matt and Mark.

"Any luck Matt?"

"Yeah, I got one room at... 213. And, almost done, the other is 241."

"So the same floor, just spread out? Great," Rachel said sarcastically.

"Don't worry, we'll be fine," Mark assured her. "By the way, Matt, how did you know how to program the key cards the rooms?"

He came around the front desk and said, "I didn't. I just fucked around on the computer and got lucky."

"Good for you. Using your brain and just getting lucky is just like magic," Mark said patting him on the back.

We walked to the elevators that were still functional. We went up and in a disoriented voice the elevator said, "Second floor." The door opened and we walked out looking for the room Matt, Rachel, and I were going to be sleeping in. We found it and Mark told us to have a good night sleep and we told him the same. Matt put the card in and the door lock flashed green to signal it was unlocked. The room was still clean and cool and surprisingly big.

"Okay, no one gets on the beds until we take bath. That still works right?" Matt asked.

"Yup!" Rachel yelled from the bathroom.

"Okay, so we do this from oldest to youngest," Matt sad

"That's only because you're the oldest, jerk! Rock, paper, scissors should decide," I said.

"Sorry guys, ladies first," she said closing the bathroom door and locking it.

When we all were showered we turned on the TV to see if there was any news. Matt flipped through the channels and he snickered and said, "Just like every other time in my life, hundreds of channels and nothing on. Fan-fucking-tastic. Maybe there's some pay per view we can order…"

I was looking at the map trying to see how to get to Tennessee. Matt was complaining about how there was some kind of code to watch the paid movies. I started to feel tired and I folded up the map. Rachel asked me what the plan was for tomorrow. "I guess we could sleep in. I mean its quiet here, like a ghost town. Nobody would bother us here I don't think."

"What about the bus?" Rachel asked.

"I don't think it'll come for us. And if it even did we don't know which direction it will come from."

They were quiet, "But, I still think we should head towards Tennessee. That must be where at least some of the military and survivors are," I said with a cough.

"So, I shouldn't place that wake-up call then?" Matt said.

We smiled. "I think that's our cue to go to bed," Rachel said.

"I'm going to call Mark let him know what the plan." I said.

I dialed Mark's room, and when he answered he sounded like he was already asleep. I filled him in on what we had talked about, and he agreed. He said that if we needed anything his room was just a straight shot to the left. I hung up, and got up to look out the window. It was dark and still. The only light was coming from a lone street lamp. It reminded me of the one that was by my house back in Houston. When it started to flicker, I shut the curtains and moved to get back in bed. I turned around and saw Rachel was looking at something. I sat down next to her and saw she had a picture of her and her uncle in her hand.

"Where did you get that?" I asked.

"It was in his wallet. I remember taking this. We were at the park. I was fifteen."

"He's watching you now. Protecting you from any possible danger."

"No, he's not, he's watching all of us," we both smiled and I got up. "Where are you going?"

"To bed," I told her.

"Can you sleep with me tonight?"

My mind was completely scrambled by that question. I opened my mouth then closed it. In all honesty, I was unbelievably nervous to lay down in bed with her, but I made up my mind and said, "Sure, okay."

We got underneath the covers and I turned off the lights. She slid my arms underneath her and I was glad the lights were off, because I could feel my face get warm.

"Mike?" she said.

"Yeah?"

She paused like she didn't hear me answer back, but then said, "Do you like me?"

I turned my head to her, "More than anything."

Her eyes opened, "Do you love me?"

I looked at her and said, "What was my first answer?"

I could make out a smile and she said, "That wasn't corny at all."

"What's with all the questions?"

"Because," she looked back at me, "I love you, too."

"Well, if the apocalypse does have an ending, would you like to be my girl?"

"Why wait?" She was leaning closer to me and our lips came together.

"Will you guys please take your goo goo ga ga talk outside? *SOME* people are trying to get some shut eye," Matt said.

Rachel and I busted out laughing. "Sorry bro, we'll keep it down," I said.

"Much appreciated." So we all fell asleep.

The next morning I woke up with Rachel still around my arm. There was a smell of coffee and when I looked up Matt was busy getting cups ready. He saw that I was awake and started laughing. I asked what was so funny, and he started to act like Romeo and Juliet. I flipped him the bird, but that just made him laugh even more. I sat up without waking Rachel and walked over to see what kind of coffee he was brewing – it looked like a mock brand of Folgers.

He nudged me and asked, "So what's the deal with last night?"

"Well…I guess…we are kind of thing right now." He extended his hand and, in a confused manor, I did the same thing. He took my hand and shook it as if I just got a job promotion. I laughed and he handed me a cup of coffee. I felt better than I did yesterday, and my cough seemed like it was mostly gone, too.

"Have you given it to her yet?" he asked.

"What?" I asked in curiosity.

"You know damn well what."

I looked over to her, "The ring?"

"Yes, the fucking ring."

"No, not yet."

"What are you waiting for? Time is running out from what I've been seeing."

"I don't know," I looked back to her, "I just feel like I should wait a little longer."

"Well, whatever you do, do it soon. Trust me the sooner you give it to her the least you have to worry about losing it."

"Less."

"What?"

"Less, you mean less, not least."

"Whatever, this isn't a fucking English class."

"Yeah, yeah I know what you mean," I said as I made my way to the bathroom. I stood over the toilet and started wondering if I should give her the ring today. Since we are technically going out with each other now…I could, but my gut kept telling me to wait. I tried reasoning with that gut feeling, but it only made my head hurt. When I flushed the toilet, I noticed that the water was black. It was thick enough to be tar.

"Hey, Matt…come in here a minute."

"Dude, I do not want to see your shit," he yelled back at me. I went and grabbed him and made him look at the tar-like water.

He looked at me and said, "I told you I didn't want to see your shit."

"No, look at it. That water looks contaminated. Did the water look like this when you made the coffee?"

"No, it was clear," he said. I looked for a cup and grabbed one from the bathroom counter. I dipped it the toilet water and it felt heavy in the small cup. I put my nose to it, but it was odorless.

Matt came closer and said, "I think I know what that is."

"It's not tar; I'm not sure what that smell is," I told him.

"I think that's the monster shit."

"You want to explain that a little?" I said giving him a have-you-gone-insane look.

"Back when we were separated, when I was looking for y'all, I was in the forest and I saw two of the smaller things feasting on a possum or a cat. I walked around them, but really freaked when one broke off from the feast and went over to the river. I thought it had heard me, but instead it took a dump there. It was like water was its cat litter. I think they've had so much to eat that now they are polluting the waters." I looked back at the cup and poured it out. It made sense. There are so much of these monsters that it causes the waters to be filled with their leavings.

There was a knock at our door. I went over and looked through the peep hole. I unlocked the door and Mark came in with a good morning. We took him straight to the bathroom and showed him what we had just discovered. He looked down and nodded, "Well, then the water's no good anymore. But how about the coffee, is it ok?"

Matt handed him a cup as Mark pointed at Rachel and said, "Still sound asleep, huh?"

"Not surprised after all that Nicholas Sparks talk they were doing all night," Matt said.

"The love story writer?" Mark asked looking at me, "You two got something going on, son?"

"Well, yeah."

He smiled and nodded, "She's a keeper. Just be careful with her. She's a bit fragile right now."

"I will."

"Now that that's out of the way – what's the plan big Stan?"

I took a deep breath in and then let it out, "We have to keep heading towards Tennessee. I feel like there will be more help and people to rely on there."

"When do we leave?" Matt asked.

The clock read eleven twenty-three and I told them, "At one o'clock we will leave and go back to the Walgreen's at least for extra food and water."

"May I suggest medical supplies, too? Just an extra precaution," Mark added. I agreed and added that we should all just rest until one. Mark got to his feet and headed towards the door, "I'm going downstairs to see if there might be a walkie or a radio."

"Do you need a gun?" I offered.

"No, I found one last night, but thanks."

I wondered if maybe there were people here and something happened that they had to leave there weapons. I went over to sit next to Rachel. I pulled out the drawers to see if there were any other weapons left behind. I opened one that had a Bible and there was a sticky note on it. I picked it up and read, "WE DID THIS! THIS IS GOD'S PUNISHMENT ON HUMANITY!"

I opened the Bible and saw everything was blacked out. Each line was covered by heavy, black ink. A couple pages in there was another sticky, "THE BEASTS WERE SENT FROM HELL TO FEAST ON THE WICKED!" I flipped through all of the pages all blacked out except for one line near the end. Revelations 13:1 read, "Then I stood on the sand of the sea. And I saw a beast rising up out of the sea, having seven heads and ten horns, and on his horns ten crowns, and on his heads a blasphemous name."

I thought back to New Year's Eve listening to the guy on the radio. The words "May God have mercy on your souls" still gave me the chills. I kept thinking about the possibility of all this being a work of God and if it was, what a sick, twisted sense of humor He had. If God works in mysterious ways, how could this be considered one? Pretty clear that He was looking to get rid of us.

I set the Bible in the drawer and closed it just as Rachel sat up and told me good morning. And for that moment, I forgot about the creepy notes and was just glad that she was with me.

"How long have you been awake?" she asked me.

"Only about half an hour. Do you want some coffee?" She nodded so I went over and poured her a cup.

Matt walked out of the bathroom and saw Rachel awake and began to waltz with himself.

"Ha ha, make all the jokes you want," Rachel said.

"Are you giving me permission?" Matt asked like he was a little child.

"Only if they're funny."

"Are you suggesting my humorous comedy is not funny?"

"Well, let's put it this way, if you were Eddie Murphy's limo driver and he was paying you to tell his jokes, I would take the ride and tip you extra to cut the jokes."

"Ouch, man Mike your girl is hurtful."

"You want a band-aid?" I asked as Rachel slapped me a high five.

"Oh, I see. Gang up on ol' Matthew, ay? Well, if you two were any cuter making googly eyes at each other, I would slap both of y'all on the back of your heads, just so your eyes would have to look another direction and give them a break."

"Just take all my money and get me to my destination, sir. Thank you," Rachel said.

Rachel and I laughed while Matt just had a smile to the side nodding his head. "Come on dude, we all know you're funny," I told him.

"Yeah, uh huh, okay," he said.

An hour passed we were starting to get our gear together. Matt was trying the TV again, but there was still no luck. He shook his head and turned off it off. There was a knock at the door and Mark came in soon after with his own backpack. He set it down on the bed and opened it.

When he was downstairs he found matches, DD batteries, flashlights, and car keys. I asked him what the car keys were for and he said, "Maybe we can find the car that matches these keys and drive as far as we can get." It was genius, and was enough to motivate us out the door.

We left our room keys on the front desk - old habits die hard I guess - and went to the parking garage. Mark was hitting the alarm button on the car, but it took us walking further down the aisle before it started going off. We flung open the doors to a 2009 Impala and hopped in. Mark and Matt sat up front while Rachel and I sat in the back. Mark started up the car and said, "Half a tank left."

"We should just go as far as we can and hope it gets us far enough," I told him. He nodded and told us to put our seat belts on. Outside of the garage and back on the roads, we let the windows down. I felt this could be our ticket to safety.

But I would soon find out that it wasn't just the monsters we had to fear. It would be the monsters in other people.

Part Three: Our Inner Monsters

We came to a stop at a gas station and looked around cautiously before we got out of the car. For the past four hours, we'd passed so many of the smaller creatures that we got the suspicion we were being followed. In the car, we started coming up with plans on how we could fight these creatures, so by the time we got to the gas station we had a plan. We all headed towards the door and Mark looked inside while we stood guard. He gave the all clear and we walked in carefully, back to back. Mark and I both had a loaded gun, Matt still had the axe, and Rachel had found a baseball bat on our way out of town. Rachel started banging the bat on the ground to stir up any of the little creatures – which we started calling Parasites. The sound of the bat hitting the floor was to anger them and lead them to us, that way we were on the offense not the defense. Matt counted to sixty and if none of the Parasites had come by then then we could move around and look for supplies. In the allotted minute, we were all really quiet and tense, but it came and went without anything appearing so we calmed down and started looking around.

Mark went behind the counter to look for migraine medicine and Rachel and I headed to the back to find water. The few that we found were warm, but we were grateful all the same. I set my backpack on the ground and we started to load water into my backpack. Rachel stopped for a second and looked out the window and yelled, "Guys! Someone's stealing the car!"

I looked outside and there was a guy hooking up our car to be towed. I grabbed my backpack and we ran out the door with our guns pointed at him.

"Don't even think about it," the man said holding up his own gun. "Me and my boy need all the shields we can get," he finished with a deep country accent. His head was bald on top and the little hair that remained on the sides still had some blonde in it. His eyes were as dark as a room at midnight, and a car-salesman smile spread across his face as another truck came speeding to a halt next to him. The driver had his shot gun trained in our direction, but when he got a look at us he lowered his gun and laughed.

"Brock?" Rachel said in disbelieving tone.

"Hey there, sugar," he said.

"Even after the world has gone to shit, you're still the ass backwards redneck fuck you always were!" Rachel responded.

"Whoa, whoa," the older man said, still holding his weapon. "Brock, do you know these people?"

"Yeah, them's the three musketeers, but I don't know the older fella," he answered him, walking towards our car.

"Wait a sec- I know the big, black man. Doctor Mark Stooping. What'cha doing with these teens? Huh? Playing babysitter?"

"What the hell are you doing with our car, Victor?" Mark said.

"A 2009 Impala," Brock started, "As a doctor, I thought you would be a rich enough bastard to afford something a little more... impressive."

"Now son, you can't talk to your elders in such a manor. Although, I don't think he would remember anything in a few minutes, eh? The Alzheimer's hit'cha yet, sonny?"

Mark raised his gun as did Brock's dad. I reached over and lowered his weapon, "We don't want trouble. We would just appreciate it if you would take the chains off our car."

"Or what, little Michael? You going to try for round two. I took you once and I will do it again," Brock said.

"No you didn't your boys did your dirty work for you," I told him.

The man looked at him and asked, "Is that the boy that clocked you? He looks like a buck fifty and he popped you without you seeing it coming?" Victor said, starting to laugh. "Actually, they might be useful to us."

"Like hell we will," Rachel said.

"Oh, I'm terribly sorry, but I'm the man that has your car all chained up and once we drive off you'll be left without a vehicle and no hope of getting to your destination," he said, talking to her like she was a toddler.

"He's right," Matt said. We all shot him an unbelieving glare. He continued, "Without a car we're hopeless. And you said it Mike, the more people the more support. Well, they may not be the exact support we were hoping for, but they are here…"

"We don't even know if they're going to Tennessee. How can we trust them?" I whispered over to him.

"We don't. We just have to go with how the survival game plays out," Mark said with his eyes squinting, as if he didn't even think about what he was saying.

I thought about Rachel being around Brock, about him trying to take advantage of her. But, I also had her safety to think about. I knew which ever decision I made, we were still fucked.

I looked over to Victor and asked, "Are you heading to Tennessee?"

He looked at me, shrugged his shoulders, and said, "Well, we are headed north so we will drop you somewhere in between."

I looked over to Brock, he was just standing there staring at me like a psychopath would, then over to my friends. I looked at the ground to see my shadow. It started moving slowly to the side, and knew it would get dark soon. I looked back at the man, "We're in. Let's go."

He clapped his hands and smiled with his black and missing teeth showing, "Prefect! Now you three will ride with my son, seeing as how you all know each other so well, and me and the Doc will ride in my truck. Capiche? Great, load up!"

I picked up my backpack and swung it over my shoulders. Brock had his arms folded and smiled like a viper about to bite, "Who's riding shot gun?"

No one said anything, we all just hopped in the back of the truck. "Ok fine, but don't complain when you get cold." To that, Rachel gave him the finger.

He nodded and said, "Just like ol' times." That's when I felt my blood heat up and wanted to shoot his head clear off his shoulders, but I couldn't let him get the best of me.

There were two long bags in the bed of the truck with us. The road was bumpy and uncomfortable, but we all silently agreed that it was better than riding in the front. I put my arm around Rachel as she leaned her head on my shoulders. Matt was looking ahead to make sure Brock's dad didn't do anything to Mark. I laid my head back and saw the sun setting, and despite everything that was happening it was peaceful. I patted Rachel and told her to watch the sunset, and she said that it reminded her of the times we sat on the roof drinking A&W Root Beer. I smiled and kissed her on the cheek.

The truck was starting to slow down, and we made a turn that led into a wooded area. I looked at Matt for answers, but he just looked back at me with the same questions in his eyes. We drove a little bit further and then stopped in an open field. Brock opened his door and got out and said that we would be camping here for the night. I wanted to ask why, but I knew he would only give me a smart ass answer.

We all got out and stretched our legs. Victor and Brock unloaded the two large bags in the back of the truck, which turned out to be one tent, lighter fluid, a small cooking iron, chopped wood and a couple of skinned raccoons. Matt made a joke about them being one of those doom's day experts, but I saw that remark as being more truth than a joke. Mark walked over to us and asked, "How are y'all?"

"The road was a little bumpy, but we managed alright," I told him. "Mark, do you know why we stopped here?"

"No idea."

The earth started to shake and we all held our weapons and listen to the roar of the large monsters that we named the Exterminators. We saw Brock and Victor carrying on with their business as if they knew something we didn't. "Look scared over there. Why don't y'all come over and give us a hand?" Victor said.

"But, those things -" Rachel said and was cut off.

"Those things never come in the wooded areas," Brock said. "It is as if the trees are poison to the beasts."

"And the little ones are terrified of fire," Victor added to what Brock was explaining. When I thought back to the attacks we had been through, what they were saying made sense to me. We'd never experienced an attack by the Exterminators while in a forest, and never an attack by the Parasites if we were around a fire.

"How do you know this?" I asked.

Victor made a coughing noise while laughing and said, "We watched the buggers closely to find their weaknesses. It was like watching a mystery movie and solving the case. Now, if you would stop standing there like road signs and give us some of that support y'all were talking about, we could get this done and over with quickly."

We set down our weapons and put the logs in the shallow pit Brock had dug and helped put up the tent, thinking now that maybe sticking with them wasn't such a bad idea.

"This tent is never going to fit all of us…" I said aloud.

"There's pillas and sheets in the truck and y'all can sleep in there too," Victor said.

We got the fire started from the lighter fluid and my matches. They placed the cooking iron over the fire and started cooking the raccoons. We all sat around the fire silent. Brock was staring at Rachel and with a smirk on his face. I looked at Rachel who was staring into the flames, but she looked up at me and smiled when she felt me watching her.

"So, Rachel…how have you been lately?" Brock asked her.

"Fine," she replied in a pissed off tone.

"Just fine?"

"Yes."

"I think you're lying," his smirk was now gone.

"Oh really?" she sounded more irritated.

"Oh yeah, I think it has to do with the boy right next to you," he laughed a little bit. "Yeah, is he your new dog?"

"Shut up, Brock."

"You going to walk around and just dump him like you did me, huh?"

"I said, shut up."

"No. I think you'll fuck him and then leave him broken hearted. Ain't that right, bitch?!"

"I said shut your fucking face!" she stood up yelling at him.

Victor was laughing while he flipped over a raccoon. And Brock started laughing too, "Well, bravo Mikey. Teaching your bitch to stand up for herself. A nice touch." That was when I bolted to my feet my fists balled tight.

"You better do what she tells you."

"Or what?" Brock said, now standing up.

"Oh, come on, boy," Victor exclaimed, "not before you eat your supper; you'll ruin your appetite."

The tension between Brock's and my eyes was heavy in the air. Rachel was squeezing my arm telling me to walk with her, but it took her pulling me in the other direction for me to finally walk away. She walked me back to the other side of the truck, out of view from the others. She looked at me in earnest, moving the piece of hair that was blocking my eyes to the side. She told me to take a deep breath and let just let it go. I did this until I stopped seeing everything in red.

"You know I can stand up to Brock just fine on my own," she said.

"I know you can, but I can't just sit on my ass while he talks to you like that; like you're some kind of animal."

"I understand that you want to protect me and I really appreciate it, but you have to let me fight my own battles too." I nodded my head and she kissed me saying, "Thanks for being there and for understanding."

As we were walking back, I heard something. I turned quickly and saw the truck shake. Rachel stared at me and asked what was wrong. Victor came behind me with a shotgun, and told me he saw it shake too. I pulled my gun from my pants and pointed it at the truck.

"It's a person," Victor said.

"How do you know?" I asked him.

"They're hiding from us. COME ON OUT NOW OR WE'LL SHOOT YA!" he yelled. There was no response and he cocked his gun. "I'M A COUNT TO THREE AND THEN I'LL SHOOT! ONE.... TWO...." and then a girl popped up from the back of the truck.

"Please, don't shoot, Please don't!" She pulled a little boy up next to her who started to cry.

"Shut him up!" Victor yelled, "Do it NOW!" The girl started speaking to the little boy in Spanish and he did his best to simmer down. Victor told both of them to get down from the truck, and they did it quickly. "What the hell do you think you kids are doing," he said, still pointing the shot gun at them.

"Please sir, w-we were separated from our parents. We're h-hungry and tired," the little girl said.

"Beat it! And find someone who gives a shit," Victor told them in a cold voice, "Start fending for yourselves, because you're parents are probably dead by now." The little boy covered his ears.

"Victor, they're harmless..." I started trying to reason with him. "What if they could be useful to us?" He wasn't listening, and the kids were noticeably shaking. "Stop pointing the gun at them," I said moving to push the barrel of the gun down, but instead I got hit in the stomach and uppercutted by the butt of the shotgun.

He pointed the gun back at them and said, "Go back to Mexico you little -" At that moment, I kicked his knee and he yelled as he dropped to the ground. He recovered quickly and hit me in the face with his gun. I felt blood coming down from the side of my eye. He punched me some more and I could hear Rachel pleading for him to stop.

"Don't you *ever* touch me again. Got that boy?" he said in my face, as he spit on the ground. "Brock, you want round two? Here you go." I couldn't stand and felt like I was trying to breathe through straw.

"BROCK! You deaf son? Do you want round two or not?" I heard Brock's footsteps slowly getting closer and Rachel's continued cries. I heard someone running and then a punch being through followed by a sudden drop. It was Matt trying to attack Brock from behind, but I Brock was just too quick.

Victor told Mark to keep Matt under control. He didn't say that exactly, but I won't repeat the words of that racist bastard. Brock walked slowly to me and stopped. My eyes were swollen and smeared with mud and blood. Brock grabbed me by the collar of my shirt and he whispered in my ear, "I hope it hurts, like your love." He threw me back down, then with his steel toed boots he kicked my head, like a football being punted. I saw a few flashing lights, then I was unconscious.

I woke up and noticed something weird. I was back in my bed, in Houston. The sun was shining in my room and I could hear the birds chirping. I pulled the covers off and walked over to the window. I saw Matt in a tank top taking out the trash while his mom and aunt were outside, sitting on their lawn chairs and reading books. I blinked a few times and tried to get my thoughts together. I saw my dad pull up in the drive way. I walked back to my bed and sat down. *Was it all just a nightmare?* I checked my phone and saw I had a text message from Rachel that said, "You didn't need to do that. You could have really gotten hurt." *What the hell was going on?*

My mom walked into the house and she seemed upset about something. I asked what's wrong but she just set my clothes on my desk and walked out like she didn't see me or even hear me. She left the door open which she knows I don't like, especially if it was closed before she came in. I got up to go close it and heard my dad talking to someone. It was almost like I knew what he was talking about. I walked part way down the stairs and saw my dad talking to me sitting on the couch. Then I remembered that this was after the suspension at school.

"What were you thinking son?" he asked me.

"You wouldn't understand," I said to him.

"Oh, really? Is this some kind of new teen trend? Fight someone just for the hell of it and get suspended!" he said raising his voice. "Who was it? Who did you so desperately need to fight?"

"Brock," I said quietly.

My dad blinked his eyes, "Brock Baxton? The boy dating -"

"Rachel. Yes, Dad."

He took off his glasses and rubbed his temple. I was starting to tear up. "Are you jealous of the boy?" He said in a calm voice. I shook my head and he sat next to me. "Then what is it? You can tell me."

"You just wouldn't understand," I said trying not to let me voice crack.

"I wouldn't? I have your mom, don't I? And you said I wouldn't understand? Like women are a new species and we haven't fully discovered them yet?" I sat there quiet. "To be honest, I still have yet to figure out your mom, but she cracked my code before we even started dating. Son, whatever feelings you have for Rachel you can't let them bring you down. Not her or any other girl in the world. Don't let women be the death of you. You understand?"

"Yes, sir," I said sniffling. He told me that I wouldn't be grounded if I didn't tell my mom. I gave him a smile and went up to my room. I followed myself back upstairs knowing what the past me would find when he walked into the room. Matt was sitting in my chair looking concerned and he asked me, "Why didn't you tell me?"

To which I replied, "Tell you what?" Assuming he was planning on a joke.

"About that fight Friday?"

I stopped what I was doing and went to sit on my bed and just thought about it, "It wasn't your fight."

He looked at me like I was joking, "It didn't seem like his fight either. He got his boys on you. And where was I? I'm your best friend. We go through shit everyday together and this you leave me out of?"

"Do we?" I raised my voice, "Ever since the eighth grade I felt like you left me for a better crowd."

"And look where I'm at now... Bro, we've lived on the same street since you were two. We've played tag and pretended to be superheroes and crap. Stayed up all night watching Child's Play and Dawn of the Dead. Listening to Nirvana while we thought girls were stupid. You got me and I got you."

I nodded and said, "Dude, I'm sorry. I can't get my head on straight."

"It's all good man. Just if you want to hang out more just say when and I'll move in here. Your closet's still big enough to hold me," he said, always knowing how to make me laugh.

I watched us go out to the roof and I followed again. But when I got to the top it was just Rachel and me up there watching the sunset and drinking A&W Root Beer. "I broke up with him," she told me. I put my drink next to me and she asked, "What? What's wrong?"

"I'm sorry. I knew you liked him and I just screwed everything up, but he shouldn't treat you like that."

"No, you didn't screw it up. You kind of saved me. He was a disaster waiting to happen. He was rude, never wanted to be around me. It was like I was some sort of title for him. No, I'm sorry Michael. That fight should have never happened."

I put my hand on top of hers. "All is forgiven," she smiled and we watched the sun sink out of the sky. On that day, after all the things I went through with my parents and my best friend, I realized it brought all of us together. One little moment can change how the future will turn out. My friends stuck by me that day and proved to me that they were better friends than I had thought. And I'm happy they were the ones to change my future.

I began to see a light and felt like I was flying. My midsection was in pain and my head was killing me. I realized that I was in the back of Brock's truck and that we were driving. I tried to turn my head but that just made it pound even more. I felt my head was on Rachel lap and I saw her looking down at me with the biggest smile ever.

"Hey, you're finally awake," she said softly.

"Yeah, how long was I out?" I asked in a weak voice.

"A week."

"A week! Oww," I said hurting my head and stomach.

"Don't overdo it. You had a major concussion and cracked ribs. Mark did your bandages and did his best to feed you broth and I've stayed with you since then."

"Shouldn't we be in Tennessee by now?"

"Victor and Brock said we're going to keep going north towards Canada now. We tried explaining why we needed to go to Tennessee. But they just ignored us."

I was having a hard time taking it all in, but I still had a feeling that it was all my fault. I decided to go with The Baxton's when we would've been alright right on foot. "What about the girl and her brother? What happened to them?"

"Cassandra and Oscar? They're fine. It seems your buddy made a new friend."

"They're with us?"

"Yeah, after what happened, Victor suddenly changed his mind and decided they could join us. Since then, Cassandra keeps trying to apologize and was worried that you wouldn't wake up. I told her that it wasn't her fault, and that Victor and Brock were looking for any excuse to fight and are fucked in the head."

"I'm glad they're okay. What about you? You feel okay?"

"I'm just happy you're fine. Oh, I got a surprise for you." She went into her backpack and moved some stuff around and pulled out Daft Punk's album *Discovery*. I began to laugh and started coughing in pain. "I just wanted to return this to you."

"Where did you get this? How did you get this?" I asked in excitement.

"We were in Kansas and Victor decided to go in a Best Buy for a power cooler or something and he wanted Matt, Mark, and Cassandra to go in with him, since I refused to leave your side. I asked Matt if he could find the album and voila."

"Wow, this is just too much. Thank you," I told her with the little voice I had left.

"Mike, can I ask you something?" I nodded and she continued, "I asked Brock why you fought him the first time and he said it was because you thought he beat me. Is that true?"

"Isn't it?" I asked now wondering if he actually did or not.

"He was arrogant, selfish, and an asshole, but he never laid a finger on me."

My head began to pound but I asked her, "Then who left you the bruises?"

She took a deep breath in and said, "My uncle did."

The world just seemed to stop at that moment. My insides began to shake and I said, "Your uncle, why?"

"He came home drunk one night and I made dinner for him. He started to babble something like how I was a burden in his home, so I started to yell at him to calm down and he slapped me then he punched me. And after he saw what he had done, it was like he snapped out of it and came to his senses and he promised me he would never drink again for as long as he lived." She grabbed the picture from her backpack and told me, "We took this on his two year anniversary of being sober. I had never been so proud of someone my whole life. I'm sorry that I never explained all of that, but I didn't want you to think that he was a bad guy or anything."

"Wow, I can't believe it wasn't Brock. I just knew he was an asshole and figured it had to have been him. Well, the second fight wasn't your fault either. Like you said they are already fucked. After we leave these guys, I hope they burn in a forest fire."

"I hope for that too. Especially what they did to Matt and Mark."

"What? What did they do?"

She looked inside the truck and then said, "Three nights ago, Victor planted cocaine in Matt's food. It wasn't just a little either. That night Matt started acting weird. He was twitching and kept saying his heart was going to explode. He said he felt cold, so he went over and put his hand in the fire. Mark realized something wasn't right and when he pulled Matt's hand out it was terribly burned. He couldn't sleep. He kept hearing voices in his head and having hallucinations. We kept asking him what was going on, trying to figure out what could have happened, when Mark saw Victor laughing in the background. Mark went up to him and asked what he had done and Victor kept laughing and said he wanted to have a little entertainment. Mark started yelling and cussing at him, but Victor kept laughing until Mark punched Victor in the face. He still has the black eye. But that's when everything went in a downward spiral. Victor started beating Mark. Just pounding him over and over again. I left your side to try and stop it, but Brock held me back and made me just watch…" Tears started streaming down her face, "Victor pulled a knife out and stabbed him in the hand, and then he…and then he…shot him. He shot Mark. He's de-dead."

I was beyond rage at that point and vowed to kill them both as soon as I was able. I would make sure they felt what Rachel, Matt, and Mark did.

It wasn't too long before I was on my feet, moving slowly but still moving. I officially met Cassandra and her brother, Oscar. She tried to apologize for everything that had happened, but I told her it just wasn't necessary especially when I learned that she had been taking care of Matt.

"Well, a couple of my older brothers had issues with drugs and I learned how to treat their withdrawal symptoms. Matt only had one hit, but it was pretty big. He will be fine, it's not like he was addicted for years or anything," Cassandra said.

I was stunned that a seventeen year old knew about all that stuff, but looking at the smile on Matt's face as he looked at her I figured he was suffering more from a love bug than anything else. Later, when I got the chance I asked him about her and he said, "I don't care if cupid shot me in the ass or not, she's worth it." I was really happy that he found someone he could connect to that wasn't just a guy friend.

When we stopped for a break, everyone, except the Baxtons, decided to eat what we had by the truck. "So, Cassandra, how did y'all end up here?" I asked her.

"Well, we were raised in Childress, me and my four brothers. It's was a really small town and we were a pretty normal family. I never wanted to live in a small town, too boring, but now I would give a lot to just be able to eat at K-Bob's Steak House with my family again..." She broke off; staring at the ground until Oscar quietly took her hand, "When the monsters attacked me and Oscar were at the grocery store getting stuff for the week. It all started from a really weird thunderstorm, and well you know what they are and what they can do. We managed to get out of the store, but our home was destroyed and we never found my parents or brothers. We've been on the road ever since."

"A lot like our stories. Oscar, how old are you?" I asked.

Cassandra jumped in saying, "Oh he can't speak a lot of English. He was going to start with the dual language program when we went back to school, but guess that won't ever happen."

"No worries, Matt can help him out. He's good with kids." Rachel said.

Matt had a stunned look on his face, one that was hard to tell if he wanted to kill Rachel or thank her. But as Cassandra threw her arms around him, he said, "Sure, I can help we will just start slow."

I started to think about Mark and how he was always helping and inspiring kids in our neighborhood, so I explained to Cassandra how we knew Mark and reconnected. Looking at Matt and Rachel, I said, "Did y'all know he was keeping a journal? He was writing about everything that was going on. He told me that I should do the same, because one day people would want to know what really happened." They all smiled and agreed that I should start writing about what's going on, but I didn't take their advice until I ?

Rachel was still thinking about Mark and remembered the time he sang at my fifteenth birthday. She loved the song so much that she later asked him who the artist was, and to her amazement he was the one to write the song. "Do you remember it?" I asked her pleadingly.

"I do." I looked at her encouragingly and she gasped, "No, I can't…"

We all started begging her, telling her that it would be in Mark's honor. "Okay, okay…"

When she started to sing we all agreed it sounded like angels slow dancing. These were the lyrics composed by Mark Stooping:

Every time the moon is full

Every day when it is cool

Just know that the day was made for you....

How can I describe how tulips grow?

How can I show the ocean's flow?

This place was made for you don't you know...

And when the time to say goodbye

To mom and pop

Always know, that they're door, is never locked.

I see you've met your lover,

You met her way back, when it was summer.

Just know that she was made for you, my brother...

And now you've grown and have wonderful kids.

They want to be just like you

When they get big.

Just let them know

This world

Was made for them.

She sung the priceless song just as beautiful as Mark did that birthday of mine so long ago. I know, wherever he is, that he has a big smile on his face after hearing that. I had smiled until I caught sight of Victor and Brock and then I could only think about getting away from then before someone else I loved got hurt. I just needed one more night to recover (I was getting more and more stable every day), before we could finally take off on our own.

I was still having trouble breathing through my healing ribs, but I woke up to my air being cut off completely by Victor's foot on my chest and throat. "Now, now, calm down. We don't want you to wake your friends. Here's the deal, my boy here is going to uh "take care of your girlfriend" to put it nicely. Mmkay? Then we're going to kill your black friend and the Mexicans, too. And since you're our favorite we are going to give you a front row seat and save you for last. Got it?" Just then, Brock grabbed Rachel's arms muffling her screams with his other hand.

"Please, don't! Just don't do this! You don't have to do this!" I struggled to plead with him through his boot on my throat.

He picked me up and threw me out the truck, knocking the little bit of wind I left in me. He jumped on me and yelled, "You punched my son, your bitch insulted us, and you're babysitter gave me a black eye. Eye for an eye, ay?"

I looked up and saw Matt come behind him with an axe, "You forgot one thing you sick son of a bitch. You forgot when I took your leg." He swung the axe hitting Victor in the back of the knee. He wailed in pain letting go of me instantly. I started to cough furiously and crawled away as fast as I could. Brock who had already tied up Rachel, was trying to pull his pants back up when Cassandra hit him in the back of the head with the cooking iron.

Brock stumbled and fell to his knees, but still conscious, "You BITCH!"

Cassandra ran over to cut Rachel's ties. As soon as she was free, Rachel, infuriated, kicked Brock in face sending him reeling back. "Now, I've been wanting to do this for quite sometime," Rachel said taking the cooking iron from Cassandra. Brock kept whimpering and Rachel slammed her foot on Brock's knee, pinning him in place, and said, "Shut your fucking face, you maggot. What I'm about to do will not and cannot be healed. The redneck bastard that you call 'Pa' gave birth to you, and I'm going to make sure you won't have the ability to ever have any kids like you or him."

She stood on the knee she stomped on, raised the cooking iron above her head and slammed it down on his testicles thirteen times. She later told me that thirteen represented how many weeks she went out with him. His pants ran red and he passed out after the first few blows.

As soon as I was able to breathe, I went to her and pulled her into a fierce hug. "Are you alright?"

"Never better." I smiled at her relieved and then turned to Matt who was standing over a legless Victor.

I put my hand on his shoulder and said, "You don't have to kill him..."

Out of breath, he laughed and said, "Oh no, I definitely do. I'm just taking a break is all."

"You all w-will die, I will fucking ma-make sure of that," Victor said stuttering out of the sheer pain he was in.

"Really, you would want to hurt us, Mr. Baxton?" Matt said in a baby voice. "Well, I guess you got too hyped up on cocaine that you didn't even bother doing anything about me. Thought I was still doped out huh?! You killed Mark, beat up my best friend, your shitty son tried fucking my other best friend, and you drugged me for your entertainment. Nah, I will fucking make sure you burn in hell."

He brought the axe down on Victor's chest. He yelled out in agony, especially when Matt wrenched the blade free. Matt brought the axe high above his head and, with a wicked smirk on his face, brought it down on Victor's, neck severing his head from the body. Matt wiped off the blood that got on his face, and said, "Well, there's one less evil thing to worry about now."

We all stood still, frozen in the shock of what we just went through. I breathed as deeply as I comfortably could and said, "Rachel, go grab as much of their gear as you can. Cassandra, go check on Oscar. Matt, help me start working on getting the car off the tow truck."

We all started moving, slowly at first and then feeling a sense of urgency that pushed us faster. Working the car off the truck, I didn't hear Brock until he had crawled within a few feet of me. "Thomson, I will kill you. You and your fucking bitch," he screamed, like a little girl, wielding a knife that he was aiming at me.

Without a second thought, I pulled my gun from my waist and shot him in eye. "Don't call my girlfriend a bitch."

The girls and Oscar came running with the gear when they heard the shot. But Matt, having just unhitched the car, told them we were fine and to get in the car. We drove off and didn't look back. There was no need to. What was done was for the best and was done for Mark.

Part Four: The Sapphire Ring

Matt drove the truck with Cassandra and Oscar and Rachel and I drove the Impala behind him heading back south. Rachel was messing with the car radio hoping to hear some kind of voice. I suggested using AM stations. She switched it over and automatically got a station with a high pitched ringing. She switched it fast and caught a voice. She slowly turned it back to the left and we heard a male voice that said, "This is a Public Service Announcement... We advise people in access of transportation to make their way to the nearest coast line. Again, if you are in access of transportation you are advised to head towards the nearest coast line."

"Why the nearest coast line?" Rachel asked.

"Ships, boats trying to get off land – maybe there aren't any monsters out at sea," I said, as I honked my horn and turned my left blinker on. Matt started to slow down, went off to the left, and stopped the truck. We all got out and I pulled out my map. "Rachel got someone on the radio. He said to go to the coast line. That was all he said though. I'm guessing they have boats to get off land." I unfolded the map, "We're about eighty miles or so from Hot Springs. If we drove for the next fifteen miles there should be a road that will take us to the east coast. How much gas is left in the Ram?"

"Little more than half a tank," Matt said.

"Then we'll all just drive the rest of the way in the truck. The Impala's is just about out," Rachel said.

"Just let me get my backpack and we'll head out." I went to the car and reached in grabbed my backpack. When started walking back, I heard the faint sound of wings and pulled out my gun and looked around. I couldn't see where it was coming from though. Then there was a shadow falling around me and I looked up to see a Parasite coming down on me fast like cannon ball. I tumbled out of the way, but as I did my bag caught on something and ripped open. I saw the ring box fall to the ground and the Parasite landed on top of it.

Matt ran towards me with his axe, "Mike, get in the truck!"

"The ring, Matt. It's underneath the bastard..." I yelled as I scrambled to my feet heading back for the box.

"Dude, we'll find another one! Holy shit!" Two more of the Parasites came from behind us and Matt swung wildly with his axe to ward them off.

When the first Parasite randomly took to the air, I dived for the box, stuffing it quickly in my pocket. Getting quickly to my feet aiming my gun, the rest of the Parasites flew off as well. "That...was odd," I said.

"Maybe they're scared of us?" Matt said.

"Doubtful, but whatever man let's go," I said, starting to run back to the truck.

Back in the truck, the sound of jets reached our ears. Swerving back onto the road, feeling the truck shake from the power of the jets, we watched the jets fly over wondering what their purpose was.

But then ground started to shake. Oscar, turned around in his seat, started to scream. An Exterminator was coming out of the ground and heading straight towards us the road cracking all around us. The jets were circling around and firing at the giant Exterminator. The beast let out a roar that made the windows crack on the truck. Matt made a sharp left turn and went off road. The ground was bumpy and made us jump when going over the small ditch. He made a quick U-turn to get us back on the road; the Exterminator was now in front of us. I saw the road up ahead we needed to turn on, but it was being destroyed by the jets' firing and the Exterminator's thrashing.

Matt sped up, a determined look on his face, weaving in and out of debris and explosions. The turn was coming up, but was blocked completely by rubble. "Hold on!" Matt yelled. He cut across to the road, catching air as we left the road and hit the ditch. The truck spun out when we hit the pavement, the back tires still spinning wildly, but Matt turned into the spin and took off when the truck was back in his control. I looked back and saw the Exterminator was running towards us, but would never catch us.

We all let out a huge breath of air and I asked Matt, "Where did you learn to drive like that?"

He smiled, "Saw it on the movies."

We drove for five hours before Oscar started crying for something to eat, and, saying in Spanish, that he needed to use the bathroom and wanted to go home. It was sad that we couldn't do anything about the last request, but we could make sure he used the restroom and got something to grub on and told him we'd stop the next chance we got.

Not too far away, we saw a sign that said, "Buc-ee's! Take the next exit!" At the store, Matt parked right next to the door just in case. Oscar went with Cassandra and Rachel to the restroom while Matt and I looked around the store for any food. There was plenty of food left, so we grabbed as much as we could. We walked back to the truck and unloaded the food in there. Matt told me to stay by the truck while he went to piss. When I got settled in, I looked to see Rachel and Matt talking. Rachel looked like she seemed confused, but then I would be to if Matt was trying to tell me something while bouncing around on his tip toes like a little kid needing to urinate. He finally gave in and ran into the restroom.

Rachel came into the truck laughing. I asked her what Matt was saying and she said, "He told me you had a surprise in your pocket."

"What!?" *Why would tell her about the ring,* I thought.

"Yeah, he said you almost died trying to save it or something," she said giggling. I looked down and felt depressed, I wanted to wait for the perfect moment not now in front of a Buc-ee's of all places.

"So, what is this super special something?"

I licked my lips and reached in my pocket. I brought it out, she looked at it then back at me, "See, the plan was to ask you out New Year's Eve with this." I held up the box, "But things kind of got hectic, so I decided to hold off and give it to you later."

"But what if there wasn't a later?"

"For whatever reason, I knew there would be and I wanted to wait until we were alone."

She looked all over the truck and then looked at me, "We seem to be alone."

I looked into her eyes and tried to remember what I was going to say to her, but for the life of me I couldn't come up with anything I had planned to say. So, I improvised, "Rachel when we first talked, I knew there was some kind of magic. I watched you go from a shy girl, to a fascinating, outgoing, kick ass woman. So, I wanted to give you this and ask...well...Rachel, will you go out with me." I opened the box and saw her eyes widen and then start to water up.

"Is that a sapphire? My-my birthstone? In a ring," she asked choked up. I smiled and nodded shyly, but she grabbed my neck and pulled me in for a kiss. But this time, the kiss was powerful;

like no other kiss that we had shared before. There was passion in this one.

"Uh, Mike, I think we have an audience."

I waved my hands for them to come on in, and Matt told us that he taught Oscar a new phrase in English. We looked at him and he asked Rachel, "Did he go to Jared?" We all laughed and started digging into the junk food.

There were two abandoned cars parked around the back of the store, so we drove back there and used a garden hose to suck the remaining gasoline out of them. We cut the hose short enough to make it easy to get out, but long enough to reach both the car and our truck. Matt was able to fill the truck's tank almost completely.

Part 5: The Beach

We were able to fill the tank up a couple more times along the way, and finally it ran out of gas when we reached California. When we walked into a town, there were people, people everywhere filling the streets. We were in complete shock seeing more people now than we had since the start of this whole thing. They were all heading in the same direction, being pushed along by different military branch soldiers. Rachel pointed out the patches on their sleeves; Marines, Navy, National Guard, and some I didn't recognize.

We continued to walk with the crowd of people. Oscar said, "¡Mis pies están cansados!" Which Cassandra said meant that his feet were hurting. So, Matt picked him up and sat him on top of his shoulders. Soon, Oscar began to yell, "Boat!" It took more walking before we able to get a good view, but past the crowd there was a boat large enough to be a cruise ship. I kept thinking of all the things that could go wrong like a mutiny or the ship being attacked by the Parasite in the middle of the ocean and sinking the ship, but I just kept quiet.

As we got closer, I could see the name of the boat was *Mercy Mary*. I held Rachel's hand tighter. I had never really felt claustrophobic, but being herded onto the boat like cattle was starting to get to me. The soldiers wanted us to board the boat two by two, like it was Noah's ark or something. Matt had put Oscar down and had his hands around the scared little boy's shoulders with Cassandra right next to him. We started hearing arguing up ahead and I realized that they were separating people onto two different sides of the ship.

When we got up to the men, they looked at us for about three seconds then directed Matt, Cassandra, and Oscar to one side and me and Rachel to another. There were too many people trying to board the boat for us to stop and complain, but I didn't want us to be separated. Matt saw the look on my face and yelled out, "We'll be close. Find us later!" I couldn't believe that we were being separated from Matt once again.

We followed a crowd of people that looked more terrified of what might happen on a boat then what could happen around the Exterminators. We were led into a room filled with chairs and more people with uniforms and were seated at the edge of a row. The room was filling quickly, which made it even warmer, and when there were no more seats the doors closed. No one made a noise. It was silent enough to hear the water hitting the side of the boat. I looked around and estimated there were about a hundred people in the room.

Ten minutes passed and I could feel the tension in the room. There was a man about four rows down who was rocking back and fourth, like he was going stir crazy. He suddenly stood up cutting off his rocking and walked heavily to the door. His wife tried to stop him, but his eyes were already lost in the madness.

He approached the men in uniforms and said, "Now you listen and listen to me well… I want answers. Why are we on a boat? And more importantly, why are we in this room waiting around like sitting ducks?" The soldiers just stared at him. "It's either give me answers or I'll bust both of your fucking skulls in. Eh? We're all tired and I can't stand waiting any longer. Are you listening you cock suckers? ANSWER ME!" he shouted loud enough for it to ring around the room.

"Sir, please return to your seat. Your answers will be answered soon, just stay calm-" one of them tried saying.

"No not soon now you mother fucker!" the man shouted again.

Thankfully a man in a lab coat, with thicker glasses than his hair, opened the door and came in the room. He looked tired, but when he looked at the irritated man he gave a small smile and held out his hand wanting him to take a seat. The irritated man stared at the man in the lab coat and then returned to his seat and his wife put her head on his shoulder.

The man in the lab coat took off his glasses and looked at his shoes. It looked like they were made from alligator hide. He looked up, took a breath in, and spoke in a deep voice, "You have questions, I have plann to answer your questions. All of them." He looked around at the people who were eagerly listening to him while he walked towards the front. "What is going on here is bigger than just this area. What is going on can be explained not as an attack, but as an invasion." The room was still as he continued on, "The first encounter was the strongest and completely wiped out the city's population. Now Paris, France is no more. Along with areas in Korea, Nigeria, Germany, and even America's own Atlanta, Georgia. These creatures answer the question about whether we are alone in the universe or not. But we didn't expect this. Many thought it would be tall, gray beings with large black eyes, but never did we think of huge monstrous creatures that have the power to wipe a country in little to no time."

"Where did they come from?" someone yelled out.

"These things were from outside the Milky Way in another galaxy which we have named Praeter Lumen which is Latin for Beyond Light. These creatures seemed to have arrived in the form of clouds and when they have accepted and internalized the earth's air pressure they shoot down like lighting." This made my stomach turn upside down and my heart sink.

"So far, there are about seven types of the monsters that we can distinguish. There are the smaller ones that fly and have a sharp tail which can make things swell up and disintegrate. The one with spikes from its bottom jaw and leading down its back are the slowest of the bunch, but no less deadly. There is a centipede-like one that uses the underground as an attack advantage. The four-toed being is also slow, but has a tongue that is long enough to wrap around the leaning tower of Pisa. There are ones that can

111

walk upright on their back legs, larger ones that were the death of the president and vice president, and one just encountered today that has a tail like a lion but is as tall as the Eiffel Tower with a speed of a smaller creature.

The room was filled with silence. No one breathed. Rachel's hand began to tighten. Then a woman broke the silence, "Are you a scientist?"

He gave a smile that looked forced, "You can say that. I'm terribly sorry for not introducing myself. My name is Allan Richardson. I worked – or I should say used to work – for NASA."

"Why are we on a ship?" someone near me yelled out.

"To be out of reach. There have been no reported attacks on water."

"So far," the irritated man yelled out.

Allan Richardson let out a sigh and said, "You are correct, so far there hasn't been an attack on water."

"Then why risk it. There are about a thousand people on this ship. And you are willing to risk their lives?" the irritated man said.

"We are willing to try anything. This was the one of the last options. Our attempts to kill the creatures from the ground and air have only been minimally successful. There is still one more option being decided on."

"What is it?" someone yelled across the room.

"I cannot give out that information. It is against our regulations."

"Regulations?!" the irritated man shouted. "We are being wiped out all over the world and all you care about is your goddamn regulations? We have all lost someone that was important to us and, buddy, I don't give one flying shit about your regulations. It's either you tell us or I will set this ship on fire."

"And if you do that, then what? Watch a thousand people on this vessel burn to death. Be left alone to deal with this madness? That's your wife next to you, huh. Do you wish to put her in more peril?" He waited for an answer, but the man just sat back and folded his arms. Allan Richardson looked around and saw we were all frightened.

He then looked at the men in uniforms and let out a breath, "The last option is to drop a hydrogen bomb in each city with a creature in it. If you are wondering if we have enough for each city the answer is yes. After the Vietnam War, we've been steadily supplying our country with weapons of mass destruction. Never knowing if we would use them or how we would use them. This might be our only hope of ridding ourselves of these monsters, but the risks are gravely high and it is not a decision to be made lightly."

The room seemed to grow colder and Allan Richardson checked his watch and took a breath in, "We have arranged rooms for everyone. We know that there might have been others that were with you when entering the ship. You may reconnect with them and find rooms together or near each other. There is a dining hall with food and drinks to your left. Eat well and drink well. Thank you all for you cooperation." He walked back to the door and the men in the uniforms followed. We all got up and headed towards the dining hall. My hand was still holding Rachel's tightly, not caring if my palm was sweaty or not, I was just not willing to lose her in the crowd.

We entered the dining hall and looked for Matt and the rest of our group. They hadn't made it in, so Rachel and I decided to wait for them to arrive before eating. We picked a table and sat down. It wasn't long before we saw them coming in from the other doors. Matt caught sight of us and they joined us at the table.

"Were y'all being lectured about the seven monsters?" Matt asked.

"Pretty much. Did they tell y'all about the possibility of the hydrogen bomb?" Rachel said.

"Yeah, pretty scary shit."

We were scared, our silence indicated that, not about the seven beasts, but about the pitiful choices our world faced just to survive.

We ended up eating a huge meal and all the sodas were gone, but there was still a little sweet tea left. The boat had left the dock and we were told we were heading towards Hawaii. We were escorted to our room which wasn't too bad. I had never been on a ship before that had beds or even plumbing. There were two beds and a couch that had a pull-out mattress. We even had our own bathroom. Looking at the tub, Oscar told Cassandra in Spanish that he wanted bubbles. Cassandra said there were no bubbles, but when Matt pulled open the cabinets he found bath bubbles. "Just don't get them in your eyes, kid," Matt told him. Cassandra beamed at him and kissed him on the cheek. He let out an, "Aww shucks," just like Goofy would say it.

Rachel was unpacking the supplies we had left in our backpack. There were still a few of shirts that were mostly clean and she gave two of them to Cassandra to have. She thanked her and said she was going to get showered and help her brother in the bath. She also mentioned washing her clothes.

"How are you going to wash your clothes?" I asked.

"Just in the sink with hot water and the bar soap. I'll just have to scrub them really good, but it will be better than nothing."

Rachel started laying out the rest of the shirts we had and said that we should all wash our clothes like Cassandra, especially our pants since we never found extras of those.

It didn't take Cassandra too long to finish up, and she came out with her hair wet wearing the T-shirt Rachel had given her. It fitted her long, but it worked out since her pants were drying on the shower rod along with Oscar's clothes. Matt was up next to take a shower and as soon as he closed the door Rachel unleashed her questions on Cassandra.

"So, Cassandra, you and Matt?"

"Yes?" she said with a confused look on her face.

"Oh, come on, I know you have a thing for our Matty."

"Since when did you become Hitch?" I asked Rachel.

"Shut it Mike, this is lady talk."

"Are you saying I like Matt?" Cassandra asked, now blushing.

"Yes. I am."

"Well," she let out a soft giggle, "I think he's cute… Wait does he like me?"

"Maybe he does, I'm not talking about him I want to know if you, the girl, like him, the boy?"

"I don't know-" she said, her now face fully red with a huge smirk.

"Yes or no sweetie."

"Yes, alright, hehe, yes."

"Sissy likes Mr. Matt," Oscar said taking a breath after each word.

"Oh, you don't have to call him Mr. Matt, doofus or dodo would be fine," Rachel said patting his head.

I started to laugh and Rachel asked me what was so funny and I told her, "You should start a match making business while on this ship."

"Well, so far my magic has worked on two couples, so I should be a billionaire by the time we're in Hawaii."

"Two couples?" I asked.

"Yes, you and me and Matt and Cassandra."

I owed Matt for the stunt he pulled at Buc-ee's with the ring, so when he came out I said, "Matt, Cassandra likes you. Ask her out. Now."

Rachel turned to me hitting me hard on the arm, but I just shrugged my shoulders and said, "Hey it's the end of the world we don't have time for this eHarmony bullshit."

Matt looked at us with a questioning face and then at Cassandra. She looked totally embarrassed, but he took her hand and asked, "You want to go steady?" She smiled and nodded. "Awesome," Matt said kissing her hand.

"That was beautiful," Rachel said smiling.

"Really powerful. Truly, this is what dreams are made of," I said, as Rachel shoved me on the bed with a laugh and an eye roll.

I felt the gentle rock of the ship as we slept. It was calming, so calming it even made me think this could be our ticket out of this mess. When I woke up, it was almost seven, about the time the sun was coming up. I looked to my side and saw that Rachel was still asleep. On the other bed, Cassandra and Matt were still sleeping too. Oscar was on the pull-out bed and if I couldn't see his chest rising up and down I would have guessed he was dead.

I got out of bed and walked over to the bathroom. I looked in the mirror and just got frustrated with my reflection so I moved on to pee. But after I was done, I looked in the mirror again something had to be done. I started looking in the cabinets and the bottom drawers and finally found what I was looking for…a pair of scissors.

I grabbed my long bushy hair and did my best to comb out all the knots and tangles. Once that nightmare was over with, I grabbed the last three inches of my hair and began to cut. Then, I grabbed the next three inches and began to cut that, and so on. When I was done, I looked my head over critically and decided that I didn't do too badly. It was a whole lot shorter and it felt a lot cooler on the back of my neck. My hair was like a before and after of Tom Hanks in *Cast Away*. I threw away the chunks of hair and rinsed my head under the sink, enjoying the cool water on my neck.

I walked out of the bathroom still rubbing my hair down with a towel to get it dry. Everyone was still sleeping and looking at Rachel I could see the sapphire ring on her hand. It was a good feeling knowing that in some ways she was mine. Looking at my own hand, I could see the soon-to-be scar where I cut myself with that piece of glass. The stitches must have been taken out when I was unconscious. It had healed pretty well, much to my relief.

I didn't want to wake anybody so I stepped outside the room and went to watch the waves. I had never been on a ship, so I only had movies to compare that experience to. I never thought something so huge and seemingly endless could be so peaceful. The wind was blowing, but not so much to be bothersome. The water was a dark blue, and it was nice not to have to worry about being attacked for once so I could just enjoy the quiet.

The only ocean I'd been around was Galveston beach, where my parents took me one summer when I was little, but that water is as brown as coffee shit. I wish my parents could see this. I began to feel sad again, but there was an acceptance to my sadness now knowing that they are truly gone. Their deaths were a tragedy that I prayed for vengeance for. I hoped that if the government or whoever was in charge would drop a bomb, then we could just obliterate the bastards.

I stood out there for a good ten minutes and decided to go back inside. When I walked in. Oscar was sitting up rubbing his eyes. He looked at me and said, "Good morning. What happen head?"

"Oh, I cut it." He didn't ask why on the account that he was still half asleep. This was the first real night's sleep any of us had had in a while. He was a strong little boy and blessed that he had a sister that looked after him.

He got up and went to the bathroom, and when he shut the door Cassandra woke up. She sat up and stretched and then looked at me as I was going to sit next to Rachel. "Your hair…" she said in a soft voice.

"Good morning to you too," I told her.

"Sorry, good morning. What happened to your hair?"

"I'm going bald. This is just the beginning," I said, as her eyes grew wider. "I'm just playing with you. I cut it early this morning."

"Oh," she said sounding like she too wanted to go back to sleep, "Where is Oscar?"

"In the bathroom." The toilet flushed then and he came out.

"Did you wash your hands?" she asked her brother.

"Si," he said.

"Okay. Are you hungry?"

"Si."

"I'll take him to the dining room. I'm hungry myself," I told Cassandra.

"You sure? It'll just take me a few minutes to get ready."

"Yeah, you can stay with Matt and Rachel. If they wake up tell them where I'll be."

"Okay, thank you."

I waved my hand to say don't mention it and got up to get my shoes on. Cassandra got up to get Oscar's clothes and help him into them. He was struggling and said he wanted to do it himself, so she let him. When he was all dressed, and we walked out the door with Cassandra telling him to stay with me the whole time.

I started talking to him to keep his mind occupied, "How old are you?"

"I am six, but seven very soon," he replied in English, which was coming along quite well.

"You know, Matt has been my best friend since we were smaller than you. Do you like him okay?"

"I like him very much. Are you marry to Rachel?"

"No, we aren't married, but she is my girlfriend," I said laughing.

"But you are like my parents act..."

"What do you mean?"

"You hold hands and kiss lips and all very gross."

I let out another laugh and told him, "Kid, I used to think girls were nasty too, but one day you will start to find girls..." I tried to find the right word, but couldn't so I settled with "pretty." He responded with a gesture that made it look like he was gagging.

When we reached the dining hall there was an orchestra playing and a few people in there. They seemed to be calm and very relaxed. We walked up to a server that had a wide smile and a badge on that said, "Ask us what's new to eat!" He also seemed to be in a peaceful state. "Hello, would you like to try the egg dumplings this morning?"

"Uh, no thanks, could we have five plates of eggs, bacon, and waffles to take back to our room?"

"Of course you can. What would you all like to drink?" I knew that Matt, Rachel, and I preferred orange juice and I told him so, but point to Oscar for a drink choice for him and Cassandra.

"I want water and my sister also," Oscar said.

"Thank you for your help," I said.

"You are most welcome, gentlemen," the server responded.

"Um, do you know when we will be docking?" I asked him quickly before we left.

"I don't. The captain did not give a specific date that we would be arriving to the islands."

"Islands? I thought we would all be on one island?" I asked.

"No, this is only ship one of fifteen. All of the cruise ships carry at least two thousand people on board. We never had word of what the remaining population would be on any one of the islands, so the higher authorities thought it would be best to spread out everybody."

I was surprised someone would have thought of spreading out the population of survivors. I told him thanks again, and he told us to have a good day. We went back to the room and I knocked with my foot. Cassandra opened the door and we entered setting the tray on the table.

Matt was awake and said "So, your girlfriend has already made you tear out your hair, huh?"

"Yeah, yeah." I looked to my bed and saw that she wasn't there, "Where is she anyways?"

"In the bathroom, I think she's sea sick," Cassandra told me.

I heard the bathroom flush and heard the sink running. I held out the orange juice when she walked out. Her hair was in a ponytail and she looked exhausted. She looked at my hair and giggled. She put her hands on top of my head and rubbed her fingers through my hair. She took the orange juice and had a little sip. "I hate being on ships, they always make me feel queasy and nauseous," she said groaning.

"So, does that mean you don't want your bacon?" Matt asked.

"Take it."

"Maybe you should rest a little longer. I asked the server when we would be arriving and he didn't know, so don't feel like you need to get ready right away or anything," I told her.

"Oh, that makes me feel tons better," she said sarcastically. I kissed her on the top of the head and helped her back into bed. When she was settled, I got a cool cloth for her head and she mumbled her thanks as she fell back asleep. She lay back down and I went to go get her a cool towel. I went and laid it on her head. She mumbled a thanks to me as she was already drifting back to sleep.

"You're so sweet to her," Cassandra said.

"Actually, there's a difference between being sweet and being pussy whipped. I think you are witnessing option two," Matt said, throwing away his plate.

"I'm sorry, did you say something stupid?" I said to Matt.

"Yes, you make Ryan Gosling look like a douche bag that wears wife beaters."

"Don't be mean Matt, I actually like Ryan Gosling," Cassandra said scowling.

121

"I've always thought about what happens to celebrities when the end of the world happens," I wondered aloud.

"Didn't they make a movie like that with the Green Goblins son or some shit?" Matt asked.

"Yeah, but that was a movie. This is real life. We can't just yell 'Cut' and grab a bagel," Casandra said.

"We can dream can't we?" Matt said.

Matt, Cassandra, and I sat in the room and just talked for hours while Rachel and Oscar were taking a nap. We talked about how we might make a living in Hawaii, or if it would even be safe to live there. Cassandra said she had a friend that moved to Hawaii a while ago and said that the soil was nice enough farming and the beaches were fantastic.

All of the what-if questions got me thinking about Rachel and me on a beach and how amazing it would be to experience something like that together. I wondered how Matt and Cassandra would turn out, and if they worked out how they would handle Oscar. Would they get someone older to help them or would Matt step up and a kind of father to him. He always said he wanted to wait until later in life to have kids, but I don't think he had considered the world ending up like this either.

There were three beeps coming from the intercom followed by a woman saying, "Good day. Our arrival time for Maui, Hawaii is nine-thirty tonight. In the time of our travel, please, feel free to roam the ship. The dining room will be open for dinner at five o'clock. Thank you and have a blessed day." It was nice to know what was happening and helped us all relax a little more.

The TV in our room flashed a green light, which was yellow last night so, I grabbed the remote and turned it on. I was expecting to see an advertisement of the ship we were on, but instead it was – on every channel – a bird's eye view of the United States kind of like watching Google Earth. It was steady for a few seconds then a couple of black dots started to appear on the screen. The area with the most dots was zoomed in on until the black dots almost covered the screen. Across the bottom of the screen it said, "Target 0001 A.K.A. Topeka, Kansas – ready for launch in thirty seconds."

Rachel sat up and grabbed hold of my arm. This was it. If this plan worked it could end all this for good, but the consequences the land would suffer would be great. But all I could think was, *Please God, don't desert us now.*

The Bomb (Final Conclusion)

In that time, we were frozen. The camera began to zoom in more on the area and we saw the carnage that was happening in Topeka. There were so many Exterminators and Parasites that it made me, literally, want to throw up. Not really sure why, but I think it had a lot to do with the anticipation. There were ten seconds left and the camera furiously zoomed out to a more expansive view. My heart was racing watching the clock, "…three, two, one." There was a flash of light that lasted for about twelve seconds and we could hear the thunderous roar of the bomb exploding. The camera zoomed out even further so the black dots would be visible, but as we watched they slowly started disappearing… until there were none left at all.

It took a long time for the smoke to clear, but when it did the camera zoomed in on the area. Blessedly, there was nothing to be seen. The Exterminators and Parasites were gone. The words at the bottom of the screen said, "Target 0001 A.K.A. Topeka Kansas – ELIMINATED."

"They did it," I said, feeling stunned eyes on me. I yelled, "THEY DID IT!" Rachel gave me hug and kissed me, and I could hear the rest of the people on the ship cheering and celebrating. I saw Matt hugging Cassandra and she kissed him. She looked at him and blushed, but before she could say anything Matt returned the favor and kissed her back.

Oscar rubbed his eyes saying, "Que?"

Cassandra picked him up and said, "The monsters will be no more!" He smiled showing all his teeth and we all looked at the television again which now read, "Next Operation, Targets 0002 thru 00032 up for eradicating. Proceed for evacuating."

At this point, I couldn't say we were out of danger. Not until every single one of them were destroyed, but, until then, we were overjoyed that there was a possible happy ending to all this nightmare.

When it was dinner time, we made our way to the dining room in a positive mood that no one had felt in a long time. We walked in and most everyone else was smiling and still cheering, but there were some that didn't believe in using such a powerful force, that nearly took out a whole state, just to eliminate the creatures.

Many would have their opinions about war and how it should be resolved, my dad always said that. He also talked about how there is war and never love. But it made me wonder, if we didn't have war, we would never really figure what was worth fighting for and that is love. I've noticed this since we first ran away in Houston, when a car almost ran me over, being separated from Matt, finding Mark and him teaching me how to stay sane while this all happened, fighting with Brock and Victor...All of that made me see we need both war and love. But I wouldn't have seen all that without my friends helping me through all the bullshit. I love them dearly, and I hope nothing will separate us. Even after all this is over.

When we reached Maui it was dark. Getting off the ship and there were hundreds of Jeeps waiting for us. We were told to take a Jeep and find the Marriott Resort using the GPS. The hotel was located about forty miles south. From there, we would be assigned a safe sanctuary. They didn't explain what they meant by that, and that made me a little anxious but I also didn't think we had any choice.

We put our bags in the trunk and hopped in. Matt was our driver again and when he started the ignition the GPS started up and gave us the direction to the Marriott Resort. Matt thanked the GPS politely and drove off following other vehicles.

It took us about an hour to reach an outstandingly vast resort. There were tiki candles burning almost engulfing the resort with light, and the rest of the hotel's lights were shining bright as well. It didn't seem as if the power on the island was affected by the attack. We got out and looked around. The crowd was flowing in, and we figured we better keep up with them. There were three long lines, so we split up to see which one moved the fastest.

We waited about ten minutes until I was almost at the desk, so the rest of them joined me and we approached the lady in the uniform. She was in her late forties and her smile was a little forced. She sat in front of a computer and looked at us asking for our name and ages. We gave her our information and she typed it all in in a heartbeat. There was a beep on the computer and she explained, "You all will be receiving a replica of your birth certificates and social security cards. Also, you will be allotted a hut suitable for all of you along with three thousand dollars each."

We were stunned over the prospect of so much money, but she quickly said, "You will need to find jobs in the area and a school for the little one."

She handed us all of our belongings in a backpack and told us to have blessed lives. We thanked her and walked away, amazed. I went into the pack to find the location of our hut. When we got back in the Jeep, I typed in the directions for our new home. It loaded and Matt followed its orders.

It wouldn't be until around midnight before we arrived at our new sanctuary. I turned on the radio and heard a radio DJ say, "We have received word that all the monsters have been taken down in the United States, and it will be a minimum five years before the bombed areas can be inhabited once again. We have shipped in many powerful bombs to other countries around the world. This is a new start for our green planet, and I wish for God to bless you all, and the ones we've lost." Then the DJ put on Louie Armstrong's "What A Wonderful World."

"It's finally over. I think it's finally over," I said.

We reached our hut and it was more than I expected. There was a walk way that was lit by candles. We got out and walked over to our new home. Matt carried Oscar who was fast asleep into the hut that was plenty big enough for all five of us. The kitchen was filled with all types of food, there were three bedrooms, and two full bathrooms. There was even a sliding door leading to a neat back yard.

Rachel opened the screen door and wanted me to come see what she was looking at. Walking towards her, I could hear the waves and I knew that at least one of my dreams would come true. It was just what I wanted, and I couldn't believe this was ours.

Matt had put Oscar to bed, before we all met in the living room. "This is it," I started, "we have walked through hell, dealt with demons, and in the end, this is it." My face feeling warm, "And now that we... survived I can finally say, without a doubt, I couldn't have done it without you all. I know it seems like we have a happy ending, but, truthfully, it really isn't. We all lost someone, lots of someones, we loved and cared for. It might take time for healing, but at least we are in this together."

"We couldn't have done it all without you, Mike," Matt said. "You stuck it out to the end and kept us alive."

"You kept your promise, just like you said you would," Rachel said, wiping a tear from her eye.

I looked at her hand and saw the ring shining from the little light that was on. To think, this all started when I tried to give her a sapphire ring and was almost killed trying to give it to her later. In my head, I thought, *Was it worth it? Being that close to death only to give the one person I love the most a symbol of how much she means to me?* The answer was clear as day, and I would never regret it.

I awoke to the sun shining into our room. When I sat up, Rachel was already up and said, "Good morning."

It took me a minute to remember where we were, but then I said, "Come out to the beach with me."

She smiled and we didn't even bother with shoes, just opened the door and let the warm air hit us. The smell of the ocean was sweet and the sand was soft beneath our feet. We stopped and I looked her in the eyes. She smiled and pushed her hair out of the way. I took a deep breath in and got down to one knee. Her eyes got wider and began to water. I held her hand tightly and said what I'd been meaning to say for a very long time, "Rachel, I love you, and I just want to know… Will you marry me?"

She looked seriously at me and nodded her head and said, "Yes, yes Michael I will." I picked her up and held her tight and we kissed on the beach just like I always imagined.

I held her waist and we stared off into the ocean. There was a storm cloud heading towards us. It was lightning and thundering, but I didn't feel scared. In the end, I knew we could face anything. If there was anything left out there in the universe, we would be ready and waiting.

About the Author

J.J. Sweed was born in College Station, Texas, and lives just next door in Bryan, Texas, with his parents and younger brother. J.J. first enjoyed writing in the second grade and progressed to writing poetry in the fifth grade. Later in life, his love of horror movies and Stephen King novels lead him to write dark stories. He started his first novel in middle school and has written several short stories. *Sapphire Kill* is his first printed work.

Author's Notes

This story was six years in the making. It started off small and kept expanding. I always wanted *Sapphire Kill* to be the first book that I wrote to be published and it has been an amazing experience.

If you bought this and read through the whole thing, I give my complete thanks and appreciation to you. Thank you to the Clara B. Mounce Public Library for making my story and dream come to life. Also, I would like to thank those that had a part in this by keeping my dream alive... To my family I love you, to my best friends much thanks, you know who you are! To Samantha Matush thank you for all your hard work and dedication for making this come true, to my high school teachers for being supportive I give my gratitude to each and every one of you.

And, as I promised (Haha!), I would like to thank everyone that I work with at Target for letting me share this story with you. You've helped me contain the beast in me and put it down on paper. This is only the beginning and it will only continue to grow.

Much Love, One Love

J.J. Sweed